CINCO DE MAYO

A *Just Cause Universe* Novel

IAN THOMAS HEALY

Local Hero Press Edition

Cinco de Mayo
Published by Local Hero Press, LLC
http://localheropress.com

1st Printing
Local Hero Press: trade paperback, April 1, 2019
Printed in the United States of America

ISBN-13: 9781971445144

Cover art by Scott Story
Book design by Local Hero Press, LLC

Books by Local Hero Press

The *Just Cause Universe*

Just Cause
The Archmage
Day of the Destroyer
Deep Six
Jackrabbit
Champion
Castles
The Lion and the Five Deadly Serpents
Tusks
The Neighborhood Watch
Jackrabbit: Big In Japan
Arena
Hero Academy
The Path
Cinco de Mayo
Search and Rescue
Rooftops
Plague
Soldiers of Fortune
Just Cause Universe Compendium
Destroyer of Earth
Flint and Steel
The Club
Jackrabbit: Rinse and Repeat
Posse
Extinction Event
Rain Must Fall

Pariah of Verigo

Pariah's Moon
Pariah's War

Three Flavors of Tacos

The Guitarist
Making the Cut
The Scene Stealers

Collections

Airship Lies
High Contrast
The Good Fight
The Good Fight 3: Sidekicks
The Good Fight 4: Homefront
The Good Fight 5: The Golden Age
Muddy Creek Tales
Caped

Other Novels

Assassin
Blood on the Ice
Funeral Games
Hope and Undead Elvis
Horde
The Murder Squad (2026)
Roast Wyvern (and Other Recipes)
Starf*cker
Strings
The Oilman's Daughter
Troubleshooters

Nonfiction

Action! Writing Better Action Using Cinematic Techniques

Chapter One

Tuesday, May 5, 2020
Loveland, CO

Breezy had a spot of guacamole on his nose, and it was driving Annalisa crazy. Her need to wipe it away approached desperation. Of course, he might take that as an invitation to get a little fresh with her, and even though she wasn't opposed to a kiss now and then, she'd have died from embarrassment if it happened in front of her parents—and his mom, too. Sure, she was almost fifteen—practically a grownup—but public displays of affection were still outside her comfort zone.

Breezy's real name was Bryson, but he hated it. He'd gone by Breezy as long as Annalisa had known him, even before his powers emerged. He had the ability to generate and control the winds. He could even fly using his cape as a reverse parachute, letting his winds support him like an airy cushion.

Annalisa could fly too, and she didn't need a cape for it, either. She wore one anyway, though, because it was part of *La Capitána*'s costume. Like Breezy, she was a superhero, and like him she was *almost* official. They'd had superpowers for a few years, but they were still a couple weeks from finishing middle school, and then would come the

1

longest, most interminable summer break of all time as they counted down the days until they and their teammates in the Neighborhood Watch would attend the Hero Academy as freshmen. That would set all of them off on their way to becoming full-fledged *licensed* superheroes, eligible to be drafted by any of the Just Cause teams around the country. It was like getting picked for sports or games, but instead, you got to be a superhero.

Annalisa had already picked the team upon which she wanted to be. She was going to New York. It wasn't a done deal or anything, but ever since she'd first discovered she was super-strong and could fly, she knew New York was the only team for her. She idolized its former commander, Mustang Sally, and now Sally was an instructor at the Hero Academy. Annalisa met her two years ago when she and her teammates managed to catch a real live supervillain.

Besides her and Breezy, the Neighborhood Watch had three other teens helping defend Loveland from . . . well, to be fair, there wasn't much to defend it *from*. The most the small town had going for it was its thriving business of sending postcards and valentines from its postal code. And, of course, it was home to the Neighborhood Watch. Annalisa had founded the team with her friend Wheels, a brilliant engineer who was developing prototype prosthetic legs to get her out of her wheelchair for the first time in years.

Then there was Rascal, a skateboarder and graffiti artist who used his ability to climb up sheer vertical surfaces like a bug to tag places nobody else could reach. He could extend his power through his skateboard wheels, and could ride it along almost any smooth surface—even walls. He was barely hanging onto the minimum required grades to enter the Hero Academy. Annalisa and Wheels were helping him with his science and history classes as much as they could. That was what teammates did; they helped each other.

Annalisa had helped Hothead too, albeit unintentionally. When he got angry, his hair would catch on fire. That wasn't especially super in most circumstances, but one time Annalisa made him absolutely *furious*, and his entire body ignited. The conflagration created a distraction that allowed her to take down a supervillain.

That had been two years ago, and it was the high point for the kids of the Neighborhood Watch. They were featured as a group on the *Power Profiles* cable show and got a couple of nice articles in *Newsweek* and *Parahumans*. They even earned a commendation from the Mayor and police department as honorary crimefighters even though they were all minors and couldn't be recognized as a real superteam. Still, it was better than nothing, and Annalisa figured any good work she could do would help bolster her chances of getting into the Big Time with Just Cause New York.

Finally, Annalisa couldn't stand it anymore, and she reached out and thumbed away the spot of green from the rich mahogany of Breezy's nose. "Hey, what—"

She showed him the smear. "You're supposed to eat it, not wear it, stupid." She deposited the green glob onto a paper napkin and set it aside.

He wiped the back of his hand across his nose and then regarded his half-eaten fajita. "Maybe I used too much?"

Annalisa laughed. "There's no such thing as too much guacamole." She brushed her fingers through her hair. She cut it short for the summer in a cute curly bob that she liked so much, she thought she might keep it even when the weather turned. At any rate, it was easier to take care of and didn't tangle so much when she was flying.

"*Es verdad, Halcónita,*" Annalisa's father interjected. *Halcónita* meant *little falcon*, which was his favorite nickname for her. She knew he wished she would pick it as her superhero name, but she was set upon calling herself *La Capitána.*

"Speaking of guacamole," Breezy's mom said, "this is fantastic, Sara. Mine always turns brown right away when I try to make it."

"Mom makes lousy guac," Breezy whispered to Annalisa, his dreadlocks tickling her cheek as he leaned in to her.

"Lime juice," Annalisa's mom said. "It's easy."

The two women fell to discussing the finer points of recipes while Annalisa and Breezy stuffed fajitas in their faces with teenage gusto. Annalisa invited Breezy and his mom over for Cinco de Mayo. It wasn't a school or work holiday, so they dined in the early evening and the crickets were already hard at work in the flowers in her mom's garden. None of the other Neighborhood Watch members could come by, but Annalisa didn't mind that so much so long as Breezy was there. They were kind of boyfriend-girlfriend. At least, she was pretty sure that was what they were. They kissed sometimes, and held hands, and flew together. It was a low-pressure kind of relationship, and Annalisa was good with that. She wasn't anywhere near ready for any of the stuff they'd been told about in Health class—and actually thought it mostly sounded kind of icky.

"So what else do you do for Cinco de Mayo?" Breezy asked. "Besides eat, I mean. There was a parade earlier, right? I saw it before."

"What's wrong with eating?" Annalisa regarded her own fajita. "There's *tres leches* cake later. That's cake soaked in milk."

"That's what now?"

"It's actually really good."

"Is that, like, Mexican Independence Day cake?"

Annalisa laughed. "Cinco de Mayo isn't Mexican Independence Day. It's just to celebrate a Mexican war victory."

"Oh yeah? Who'd you beat?"

Annalisa's dad took a pull from his beer. "*Las ranas.*"

"That means *the frogs*," Annalisa supplied when Breezy looked lost. "Mexico beat the French."

Breezy chuckled. Like her, he was doing well in History. "That ain't no thing. Everybody beats on the French."

"There will be some fireworks later, over at the Fairgrounds," Annalisa said. "And . . . I guess that's about it."

"See, now that's just poor plannin'," Breezy said. "We should have gotten the day off. We get Martin Luther King Day off."

"Yeah, but that's in January. Who wants a day off in January?"

Breezy pointed at himself. "This dude."

Annalisa ate a spoonful of barbecue baked beans. Breezy's mom asked what she should bring and Annalisa's parents said she didn't need to bring anything. Breezy said his mom wouldn't dream of showing up empty handed, so she mixed up a homemade batch of baked beans with caramelized onions and thick-cut bacon. They were delicious, if not exactly traditional Cinco de Mayo fare.

A faraway look crossed Breezy's face and he stopped eating for a moment.

"What's up?" Annalisa asked him.

"Oh, nothin'. I was just, you know, thinkin' about the fall. The Academy. That's gonna be such a trip."

"Yeah," Annalisa said. "I'm glad you're going with me. Us. With all of us."

"What if we ain't good enough? What if we can't hang with the other students? We could get stuck as Champions. Or maybe even not get picked up anywhere at all. That happens. It happens all the time, Annalisa."

Annalisa reached out and squeezed his hand, hoping her parents wouldn't see. They wouldn't be upset or anything—they liked Breezy. It would be embarrassing, though, and it had been bad enough when her mom sat her down and had the sex talk with her. "It won't happen to us, Breezy."

He smiled at her, his white teeth gleaming in his dark face. "Oh Captain my Captain."

His words gave Annalisa a special little shiver in the small of her back. She wasn't sure what that meant, but she liked it. She smiled back at him and opened her mouth to follow up with something suitably inspiring.

A loud series of pops from somewhere nearby made the words back up in her throat.

"Firecrackers?" Breezy asked.

Breezy's mom frowned. "Those were gunshots. Ain't no firecrackers sound like that. Everyone get in the house. Y'all got a basement?"

Annalisa's parents looked at each other and nodded. "Yes, I think you're right, Amanda," Annalisa's mom said. "Kids, inside, right now. Leave the food."

"Mom," Annalisa began.

"No, Annalisa."

"Mamá, I'm bulletproof. I got shot two years ago and nothing happened."

"*Hija*, that could have just been lucky. Get in the house!"

"Mom! Someone could be hurt. Let me go look, at least. I'll be careful!"

"It's okay, Miz Torres. She's *La Capitána*. She knows what she's doin'." Breezy followed his mom into the house. "Come inside. We'll be safe here."

Annalisa nodded her silent thanks to Breezy. He nodded back at her, worry written all over his face the way his lips were pressed tight together. Then he disappeared into the house with the adults.

Annalisa wished she had her cape, but she didn't want to take the time to go dig it out of her room. Breezy couldn't fly without his, so he couldn't back her up. She'd have to deal with whatever it was on her own, but it wouldn't be the first time she had to be a solo hero.

She clenched her fists, strong and resolute, and leaped into the sky.

Chapter Two

Annalisa rose into the sky quickly, clearing the treetops and heading straight up to get a bird's-eye view of the situation. Being late spring, a sparse leafy canopy covered much of the neighborhood, interspersed with residential rooftops in gray, brown and beige. She could smell the smoke from dozens of cookouts, but beneath that lay the sharp scent of gunpowder.

It was a smell Annalisa knew all too well.

Two years ago, when the Neighborhood Watch fought and captured the French supervillain known as *Le Masque*, he pulled a gun and shot Annalisa. At the time, she merely shrugged off the bullet as she took him down, but much later, she came to the sober realization that she could very well have been killed. She still had nightmares about the gun going off and the sharp punch to the gut as the bullet flattened itself against her side. In her worst dreams, the bullet didn't stop, but tore through her flesh. She always awakened as she was bleeding out in her dream, and then she'd have to turn on her light with shaking fingers and try to find anything to distract herself so she might eventually go back to sleep. Anything to avoid thinking about that bright muzzle flash and the stink of burnt powder.

She was smelling it now, and she knew Breezy's mom had been correct in her initial assumption.

She hoped someone had just been stupidly celebrating by firing their gun into the air. Such a thing wasn't unheard of, because some people were idiots. Bullets came back down. One of Annalisa's classmates had an aunt who had nearly died on an Independence Day when a random bullet had crashed through her sunroof and cracked her skull.

A flicker of flashing color caught her eye and she flew in that direction until she was hovering over the park where a pair of police SUVs sat parked, doors open, lights flashing. Two officers had a man face-down on the grass. She was about to fly down to see if they needed any help but froze as one officer stood from where he'd been busy cuffing the suspect.

The suspect's back was a bloodied mess, several wounds showing through his t-shirt. He had dark, curly hair like Breezy's and skin like Annalisa's dad. It made shivers run up and down her spine. She'd heard so many times about white officers shooting minorities, and here it looked like maybe she'd encountered it for herself. The older officer who'd applied the cuffs grimaced at his hands and wiped them on his trousers. His youthful partner turned and vomited on the grass, collapsing to his hands and knees.

"Get up," the older officer said. "Get your ass up. We don't have time for this." He said something else but Annalisa couldn't hear. The older man hauled the younger to his feet and recoiled at the young officer's foul breath. "Jesus, go get a drink of water or something."

With fumbling fingers, Annalisa found her phone and touched the *video record* button. She wasn't sure what she was seeing, but she wanted to document it. She hoped she wouldn't drop her phone.

The two officers spoke in low, rapid tones. She couldn't hear it, but they kept looking toward the handcuffed man on the ground. His blue shirt had darkened with blood until it had transformed to a rich burgundy. He hadn't moved since Annalisa arrived. She had a sick feeling in her stomach that he might be dead. If he wasn't dead, the cops didn't seem particularly concerned about his wounds. Should she call an ambulance? The only number she knew to call was *9-1-1*, and the police were already there. Surely they'd already called someone.

"Check him," said the older officer at last.

"Check him yourself," retorted the younger man. He pulled his hat off and wiped his forehead. Annalisa saw he really was just a kid, maybe only a couple years out of the police academy. His head was inexpertly shaved and sweat dotted the stubble on his scalp. He looked like he might throw up again.

The older officer had the look of a man who had seen it all in a lengthy career behind the badge. He grunted as he knelt down to check the pulse of the man on the ground. Then he cursed and stood. "He's gone."

"What do we do?" cried the younger man. "Phelps, what do we do?"

"*We* don't do anything, and especially *you* don't do anything, Hembeck. Stand there and shut up. I'm calling this in. Anybody asks, he went for your gun."

The younger man looked like he was about to burst into tears. Annalisa knew how he felt. She felt tears pricking at the corners of her eyes. "Aw, no, Phelps. Don't say that. Don't make me say that."

"Shut up. You say anything else and your career is over, understand? He went. For. Your. Gun." Phelps pulled his radio from its shoulder clip and spoke into it. When he finished, he looked back at his partner. "You pulled your gun too, Rich, same as me. How many shots did you fire? Three? Four? You're in this just as much as I am. Only way we get out of this is if we get our stories straight."

Annalisa heard sirens in the distance and both officers looked in that direction. She realized how much closer she'd drifted to the men, trying to listen to their conversation. If one of them so much as glanced just the slightest bit upward, they would see her. She launched herself up and away, putting as much space between herself and the two officers as she could.

Once she was a safe distance away, she landed atop a convenience store roof and almost collapsed as she realized she was shaking. She needed to get herself under control. There was . . . a dead man—a man who wasn't white—in the park, and it looked like the police had shot him . . . and it looked like they were trying to cover it up with a lie.

Racism was an ugly word and an uglier concept, and unfortunately, it was something which Annalisa experienced regularly. As a Hispanic girl living in a largely white community, she was often regarded with suspicion. Store security or busybody personnel who decided to act as such would follow her around sometimes if she went into a store by herself. If she spent too long somewhere without spending any money, sometimes she got asked to leave. And sometimes, she got told.

If she had it bad, Breezy had it worse. Annalisa's parents hadn't ever had the conversation with her about how to behave if she was stopped and questioned by the police, although she knew they'd talked about it with the growing hatred and distrust that seemed to be everywhere. Breezy's mom had sat him down and given him some stark directions and warnings about what to do and what not to do, what to say and what not to say if a police officer ever approached him. "It doesn't matter that you're a child, or a parahuman, or if you're in your costume or not. The reality is a police officer is going to see the color of your skin first, and whether it's a man or a woman, black or white or brown, racist or not, they'll see you as an elevated threat. You don't even have to make a mistake to have a gun pulled on you. Or to be put in cuffs. Or . . . or worse."

Breezy had recapped the conversation to Annalisa in a steady monotone, clearly upset. His mother's oldest brother was shot and killed in Oklahoma City before Breezy was born just because his car had broken down and a cop got a little too concerned about the black man who might have appeared on the surface to be stealing a car instead of repairing it. Even Breezy's own father was once arrested simply for complaining about being overcharged at a Denny's. He'd long since disappeared from Breezy's life but the teen seemed to be turning out okay.

Thinking of Breezy reminded her that he was back at her house, along with his mom and her parents, and they were all worried about her after hearing the gunshots. She pulled out her phone to text him and paused.

She had recorded some important video, and she wasn't sure what to do with it. Luckily for her, she had a certified genius on her team in Wheels, and a social-media expert in Rascal. She even had Hothead, who managed to stay grounded in reality despite all their fanciful powers.

Annalisa sent a quick text to her mom to report that she was all right and there wasn't any danger, but she needed to meet up with her team. Having accomplished that task, she opened the Neighborhood Watch app Wheels had installed on everyone's phone, and triggered the emergency alert button. "Everyone, it's La Capitána. Emergency team meeting at headquarters ASAP," she said into the app. Her voice message would be distributed to all the others.

She tucked her phone back into her pocket, raised her fists over her head, and shot into the sky, heading for the Neighborhood Watch headquarters.

Chapter Three

The Neighborhood Watch headquarters had grown over the past two years as Wheels' inventions required more and more space. Her dad gave the teens a whole corner of his salvage yard to use as they saw fit. What began as a single Winnebago that the kids cleaned up and refitted into a reasonably comfortable space now included a couple of beat-up Con-Ex containers that Annalisa wrestled into place and pounded back into a semblance of square with her fists, feet, and a lot of attitude. Hothead tried to help but couldn't quite generate enough heat for his flames to act like a cutting torch. Instead, Wheels hooked up her dad's rotary diamond-blade saw and they cut doors and windows into the containers. Hothead found his abilities useful enough for sealing clear plastic sheets over the window holes to keep out the constant wind, very occasional rain and snow, and the mosquitoes that were a constant bother in the salvage yard. One container became Wheels' workshop, where she tinkered on potentially useful gadgets and the other was a garage for the team transport she was building, based upon the frame of a wrecked car.

Wheels was in her workshop when Annalisa touched down in the auto salvage yard with a satisfying thud and a cloud of dust, which was her favorite way to land anywhere. The young engineer appeared at the top of the short ramp leading into the container, wearing her old, stained fishing vest bursting with tools and welding goggles on her forehead. "Hey, Annalisa." She wiped sweat off her face with the back of her hand.

"Hey, Aighleigh. You working on your quad thingie?" Ever since her legs became paralyzed in the car accident that killed her mother, Wheels dreamed of once again running. Her parahuman ability of super-engineering most closely resembled that of the legendary supervillain Destroyer, but where he had used his tech to attack and kill superheroes, Wheels was using hers to help others. She'd spent years customizing and upgrading her wheelchair to make it into a powerful and effective crimefighting vehicle, but that hadn't gotten her closer to her goal of new legs. Over the past couple years, she'd been designing and building a four-legged rig with the help of a couple of Boston Dynamics engineers whom she emailed constantly.

"Of course. I'm not too far from a field trial. Few more hours of work and I'll be out running around. Well, sort of, anyway." Wheels rolled down the ramp and over to the Winnebago where the Neighborhood Watch still met to discuss being superheroes, watch TV, and drink Mexican Cokes.

"You know we can't keep calling you Wheels if you have legs." Annalisa held the door open for her friend.

"I'm still thinking about that. Superhero names are hard."

Breezy floated down, light as a feather, riding the parachute of his cape, connected to his wrists, ankles, and shoulders. Except for the cape, he still wore the basketball shorts and tank top he'd worn to Annalisa's party instead of his full costume. "They ain't that hard."

"Are you gonna be Breezy forever?" Wheels asked, using her chair's power assist to roll up the ramp into the Winnebago. It was hot and stuffy inside but at her arrival, the air-conditioning unit on the roof squalled to life and ice-cold air emerged from it.

Breezy gathered the folds of his cape so he wouldn't trip. "Maybe. It ain't a bad name." He looked at Annalisa. "So the cops shot a dude?"

"I think so, yeah." Annalisa frowned.

Wheels spun her chair around. "The police shot someone? Dead?"

Annalisa shrugged. "I think so. He wasn't moving and they weren't, you know, trying to save his life."

"He's definitely dead." Vinnie walked into the Winnebago, his skateboard stuck to his back thanks to his powers. He hadn't bothered with his Rascal costume either, and had on baggy cargo shorts and a thin t-shirt. "I've got a couple Ragers over there reporting on what they see."

The Ragers were Vinnie's field operatives. He cultivated a huge fan base on social media, thanks to his carefree attitude and willingness to record his graffiti escapades. By focusing his attention on local followers, he had a virtual army of eyes spread across the city, mobile on bikes, boards, and blades, ready to report in with Instagram and Twitter at a moment's notice. The prevailing belief among the Ragers was they could go anywhere, and because they were just a bunch of kids, adults wouldn't pay attention to them.

More recently, he even recruited some older Ragers, who had drivers' licenses and cars of their own.

"Where are they?" Wheels asked. Vinnie told her which park. Her fingers danced across her tablet. "I've got a cage in that park. I'll send a dragonfly to check it out." Wheels scattered small solar-powered boxes all over town, placed in hard-to-reach areas with Vinnie's help. They contained hand-sized drones shaped like dragonflies with cameras and microphones. They could run for fifteen minutes on a full battery charge and were completely reusable so long as she got them back into their cages before they drained.

Annalisa caught movement in the corner of her eye and turned to look out the window. A car pulled up by the gate of the salvage yard and a pale, redheaded boy got out. "Thanks, mom." He waved as the driver beeped her horn twice and drove away. He trotted across the yard to headquarters.

"Cole's here," Annalisa said. "His mom brought him." Cole was their last teammate, Hothead.

Wheels smiled. "At least she's supportive of him. It'd be worse if he had to ride his bike everywhere. He'd never catch up with us."

"Maybe you get the Watchmobile runnin', we don't have to worry about that," Breezy said.

"He'd still have to get here to get in it," Wheels pointed out. "Or we'd have to go pick him up." She looked up at the biggest TV on the Winnebago wall and smiled as the screen changed from a *no signal* notification to an image. "Dragonfly is on site."

The screen showed green treetops and blue sky in a wide-angle view, then swung down to a scene of flashing lights and police activity. The officers had strung crime-scene tape around the area where Annalisa had seen the dead man, now covered by a sheet. CSI-types were marking and gathering evidence, like bullet casings and, Annalisa realized, one of the dead man's shoes.

He'd been shot right out of his shoes. Annalisa's dinner came up and she barely made it to the Winnebago's bathroom in time. The others groaned and fled out the door as she heaved her guts out. After a minute, when she was sure she was done, she flushed, closed the lid, and grimaced at the sourness of her mouth. Her hands were shaking so bad she could barely get the sink faucet turned on, and she accidentally cracked one of the cheap plastic handles when she grabbed it too hard. She splashed water on her face but her eyes kept watering and she realized she was crying.

When she emerged from the bathroom, a subdued Breezy was sitting on the couch, waiting for her. He stood and handed her a Mexican Coke. "Here, I know you probably need somethin' after that. My mom always gives ginger ale for a rumbly tumbly, but we ain't got any." He lowered his voice. "When I seen that dude laid out, I didn't feel too good either." He reached out, tentative, and squeezed her hand.

Annalisa sipped at the Coke, letting the flavored bubbles swirl away the puke taste in her mouth. "Thanks, Breezy."

"I got you, Capitána. Always."

"You gonna make out right after she puked? Man, you're braver than me." Annalisa and Breezy whirled to see Vinnie lounging against the Winnebago's door frame, an insouciant grin plastered across his face. "I wish I had some popcorn."

"Jerk," Annalisa said without rancor; Vinnie was just that way and she didn't take it personally.

Vinnie grinned. "You guys oughtta start your own streaming channel. Hashtag pukey teen romance."

Breezy snorted.

The cool air from the air conditioning helped Annalisa to feel better. "Whatever. You guys can come back in. I'm okay now." She steeled herself and turned back to look at the police investigation as it played out on the screen.

Vinnie pointed to a van on the edge of the screen. "News crew." He checked his phone. "Ragers say there are three networks here already."

"Police-involved shootings are usually big news, aren't they?" asked Cole. "Besides, it's kind of a slow news day, otherwise."

"It's not going to be slow for long." Wheels sounded grim.

"Why not?" Cole asked.

Wheels turned on a second television and played the footage from Annalisa's phone on it. "Do you see it?"

Annalisa felt weak and sat on the couch. Breezy dropped beside her and took her hand in his. His skin was cool and clammy to the touch, and he was clenching his teeth so tight she could see the muscles of his jaw twitching beneath his skin. "I see it," Breezy said softly.

"See what?" Cole asked, a tiny plume of smoke rising from his scalp as he started to get angry about not knowing what the others already knew.

"The bullet wounds. They're all in his back," said Wheels.

"So?" Cole challenged.

"So he wasn't facing them," Vinnie said. "They shot him in the back."

Chapter Four

Wednesday, May 6, 2020
Loveland, CO

The police shooting was the talk of the school the next day. Half the kids were trading rumors from questionable sources, while the other half were fact-checking, noses buried in their phones and shouting about what was and wasn't fake news. Everyone had their own theories on what happened and whose fault it was. There were a few things everyone agreed upon: the victim was a half-black, half-Hispanic man named Dominic Ortega, and he'd been pronounced dead at the scene by the paramedics. The officers involved had been placed on administrative leave during the investigation.

Annalisa and her teammates had a long discussion about what would be the best course of action with her video recording. Breezy and Vinnie had been all for releasing it onto the internet and letting people's natural inclination to pile on run its course. Aighleigh was against that for the very same reason. There were too many self-styled internet vigilantes eager to destroy lives just so they could watch the carnage unfold. "It'll take them about a minute to track down Annalisa and the rest of us," she said. "Half of them will be trying to make us into figureheads and the others will be threatening us with rape and murder."

Cole agreed with Aighleigh. When they'd put it to a vote, Annalisa's tie-breaking vote had been with Aighleigh. She knew they would need to share the video at some point, but they needed to figure out the best time and way to do it. Aighleigh promised she'd give it a lot of thought, and Annalisa knew her friend would come up with a good solution.

The kids of the Neighborhood Watch actually had better information than most other kids in school, partly because they'd been direct witnesses to the minutes shortly after the shooting thanks to Annalisa's video, and partly because Breezy's mom knew the victim. Ortega's wife was one of her coworkers at her fabrics store. "My mom said he worked at the bottlin' plant," Breezy said to Annalisa as they ate limp, flavorless fries in the school lunchroom. "She didn't know why he would have been at the park, though."

"Maybe it was on his way home?" Annalisa said. "Did he like to walk after work? My folks do that, except when my dad's too tired."

Breezy shrugged. "I dunno. Could have been any reason he was there."

Annalisa lowered her voice so the other kids in the lunchroom wouldn't hear her. "Why do you think the cops shot him?"

Breezy frowned. "He was black. Cops shoot black people."

"He was half Mexican," Annalisa said. "And not all cops."

"No, not all cops, but those two cops did. And they shot him in the back. That means he was either runnin' away or he wasn't lookin' when they did him. That ain't right, Annalisa."

"Maybe they had a good reason." Annalisa didn't want to think the worst of the police. She had made a couple of friends on the local force. Officer Bickle was as tall as a tree and built like a superhero, but he was as gentle as a big dog. He was almost as dark as Breezy, but shaved his head. His partner was a short, quick-tempered Hispanic woman named Velez. She was like the angry chihuahua to Bickle's Great Dane.

"Ain't no good reason to shoot someone in the back." Breezy swirled a fry around his ketchup puddle, grimacing as the weight of the sauce broke it apart. "It's called *while black*."

"While black?"

"Drivin' *while black*. Walkin' *while black*. Even sleepin' *while black*. Cops get called. It happens. It happened to my mom in a store. Some Becky called the cops on her because she was *actin' suspicious*. She was shoppin', Annalisa, at the same damn mall where she works."

"Shopping while black," Annalisa said, feeling very small.

"At least nothin' happened to her then, because she did everythin' right and the cops let her go. She was gonna sic a lawyer on that store but then figured why bother?"

Cole sat down beside Breezy. "Hey, guys."

"What's up, Cole?" Annalisa asked.

"There's going to be a candlelight vigil at the park tonight. We ought to go."

"You think so?" Breezy asked. "Yeah, we probably should. My mom will be there, and I don't want her to go by herself."

"I'll go with you," Annalisa said. "I don't want you to go by yourself either."

"Thanks, Annalisa."

Cole rolled his eyes. "I swear, you guys are the worst."

"You can come, too, Wonder Bread." Breezy nudged Cole in a good-natured way.

"Somebody's got to be the Man keeping you down," Cole retorted. They'd had the same conversation or variations of it dozens of times and nothing made them laugh harder than the scandalized looks they got from adults who overheard them.

It was Annalisa's turn to roll her eyes.

"'Scuze me, somebody said this was the meeting for Junior Just Cause. Are we in the right place?" Wheels rolled up, her lunch tray in her lap holding the remains of what passed for salad in the school cafeteria. Vinnie was with her, his skateboard casually stuck to his back with his powers. Nobody noticed or cared about the parahumans in their midst. Everyone in the school knew about their powers but the novelty faded quickly for most students when there was the powerful draw of YouTube and Instagram.

"Junior Just Cause is at six," Cole said. "This is Fight Club."

"But we're not supposed to talk about it," Annalisa said quickly. None of them had seen the movie from which the quote was said to originate, but they'd all seen a hundred memes spouting the same thing.

The others laughed.

"Actually, we're talking about the candlelight vigil tonight for Dominic Ortega." Annalisa's statement cooled their jocularity like she'd thrown water on a fire. "We're going to go."

"I think that's a good idea," Wheels said. "We should all go. It'll do the people good to know we're supporting them. I mean, we're the town's resident superheroes, right?"

"Full costumes, then?" Vinnie said. He looked excited and Annalisa couldn't blame him. His costume was pretty cool, with pieces of armor made from melted skateboard wheels and a leering demonic mask.

"Long as it's not Laundry Day at Breezy's," Cole said, and the others laughed. The one time Breezy's mom had stolen his costume to wash it because—in her words, it smelled like a goat had been wearing it—had been the very first time the team had responded to an emergency. Nobody ever let him forget it, either.

"Yes, full costumes," Wheels said. Annalisa grinned. She and her mom had worked together to make a *real* costume, not just the t-shirt and improvised cape she'd worn a lifetime ago in seventh grade. She looked good in it, and she felt strong and powerful. She'd heard the phrase *clothes make the man*, and that might have been true for guys, but for her it was so much more than that. She'd spent her life wanting to be a superhero, and she loved to look the part. Besides, she kind of liked how Breezy's eyes bulged out of his head when he looked at her in it.

The group finalized their plans to meet up at the park and then lunch was over and they had to return to class. Annalisa had Social Studies after lunch, and instead of the regular lesson, Mr. Gilchrist moderated the class in a spirited discussion about race and policing. The discussion carried over into the hall at passing period, and in one case escalated from discussing to yelling until Annalisa pushed her way between the two arguing boys and held them apart at arms' length. "Knock it off, Derek. You too, Tyler. Or I might forget I'm not supposed to use powers against you."

The boys backed down, muttering under their breaths as they walked in separate directions.

"Yeah, that's what I thought," Annalisa said. She caught Mr. Gilchrist's eye as he stood in his doorway. He gave her a thumbs-up and a smile. She smiled back. He got it, unlike a lot of the adults in Annalisa's life. He confessed to being a bit of a superhero junkie himself, but warned her it wouldn't mean she could coast through his class. His was one of the toughest classes ever. In the end she had a high B going into the final exam, and she felt pretty confident she could bring that up to an A. She'd worked harder for that grade than she had any other class, and she was proud of that fact.

The bell rang and she realized she was basking in her own greatness, and that meant she was going to be late. Humbled by the prospect of a marked tardy on the attendance log in English, she violated school rules and flew through the hall above the few other stragglers in the halls so as not to collide with them. She was grateful the District hadn't yet gotten around to installing cameras in the halls so she could get away with it if no teachers or administrators saw her. She made it to English just as the second bell rang and slipped into her seat with nobody the wiser.

She smiled to herself. Being super was *awesome*.

Chapter Five

When she first started out as a superhero, Annalisa's costume was purely homemade. It was a green t-shirt with a star on it, jean shorts, and her mom's boots that she had to load with extra socks so they wouldn't fall off. The only real concession she made to a traditional superhero outfit in her original costume was the addition of a cape, and that was because capes looked cool when she was flying.

After she and her team busted Le Masque, her parents invested some money in materials from Breezy's mom's store and recruited her grandmother as a seamstress. They worked with Annalisa's ideas and her grandmother made her a new costume, one that made her look like a real superhero.

Her new look began with a reflective green full-body suit of a tough, stretchy fabric that was a blend of spandex and denim. She had a large white star insignia, tipped onto its side so one point went up to her shoulder while its opposite dropped to her hip. She'd decided the offset look stood out more than a traditionally-aligned star. People would remember it. They would also remember the cape, because La Capitána should always have a flowing red cape. Her boots, ordered online from overseas, and her costume gloves were both the same shade of red as her cape.

She wore no mask. Most heroes didn't anymore. It was technically illegal to do so unless one's identity was publicly known, which Annalisa's was. In the Information Age, the argument about protecting one's loved ones via a secret identity didn't hold up. Almost anyone could be identified with a few minutes of Google searches or by CCTV and facial-recognition software. It took real effort to hide one's identity in the Information Age. Beyond some local media, nobody had ever taken any interest in Annalisa's parents, and she was just fine with that.

The lack of media interest might change with her attendance at the candlelight vigil. She and the rest of the Neighborhood Watch were in attendance, lending their support and solidarity to those who had gathered in remembrance of Dominic Ortega.

Breezy's mom stood with Annalisa's parents. They joined the others in singing *Amazing Grace*. Annalisa likewise stood with Breezy, holding a candle and listening to Breezy sing because not only did she not know the words, she couldn't carry a tune. His voice was changing, and every once in a while he'd make a weird squeak and she'd smile at her candle as she hummed along, trying to participate.

Breezy was also in costume, a blue and white sleeveless bodysuit with gray swirling accents and his big blue parachute cape.

Hothead stood off to one side, not quite by himself but not near anyone in particular. His main reason might have been due to the small candle-sized flame sprouting from the top of his head instead of the unlit candle he clutched. He had grown enough in the past two years to need a new costume. His most recent version was a one-piece bodysuit of flame-retardant material, white at the shoulders and graduating through yellow, orange, red, and darkening to black at the feet. With a flame logo emblazoned on his chest, he probably looked more like a conventional superhero than anyone else on the Neighborhood Watch except maybe for Annalisa.

Rascal's costume hadn't changed since his first, a basic black suit with plastic armor pieces stuck on it using his powers. He and Wheels were together at the opposite end of the vigil. They spent so much time together that Annalisa asked Aighleigh if there was something going on between her and Vinnie. Aighleigh got all tongue-tied and blushing, so she was pretty sure there was. It made Annalisa smile to know her best friend was finding some happiness, and that Vinnie didn't appear to care that she was paraplegic.

Wheels was testing out her new quadropede. She sat on a control saddle, carefully strapped in and braced between two pairs of hydraulic powered legs. She could walk, prance, and even trot like a pony. She had said she would be developing the ability to gallop soon. Eventually she intended to cover the vehicle's framework with lightweight armor to protect it and look a little less industrial. The simple fact that she could *walk* again for the first time since the car accident had her smiling, even at the sadness of the vigil.

A police car rolled up the street, slowing as it passed by the mourners. Annalisa didn't think anything of it until the jeering started. "Pigs," someone shouted. "Shoot an unarmed black man in the back. Get out of here!"

The patrol car stopped. Its lights stayed off but Annalisa saw the officer inside watching the mourners, speaking into the radio.

"Pig!" someone shouted again.

"Knock that shit off," someone else said. "That ain't helping."

"Y'all need to show some respect," Breezy's mom said. "This isn't who we are."

Annalisa glanced at Breezy. He was frowning in the candlelit darkness. "This ain't good," he said. "Someone's gonna say something and then we're gonna have a riot."

Annalisa didn't know what else to do, so she flew up until she was floating over the crowd. People stared at her and she felt her face grow hot. She knew she should say something but her tongue was paralyzed. "Um . . ." She hated that uncertainty. Civilians looked up to her, both figuratively and literally, and she couldn't think of a single thing to say. Some hero.

"Annalisa, what are you doing? Get down!" Her mom hissed at her.

The two mourners who'd been shouting at each other squared off, still yelling. The police officer flipped on the red and blue lights and made a *whoop whoop whoop* with the siren. "Everyone please clear the area," the officer said over his car's loudspeaker. "This protest is over."

"Protest? This is a vigil," a woman called. "We have the right to be here."

"Annalisa, let's go," her mom said.

Annalisa winced. She wished her mom wouldn't use her name, even though it wasn't a secret. "I'm in costume, Mamá. Call me La Capitána. And I'm staying."

Breezy floated aloft, his cape billowing around him as his winds cradled him in their embrace. "Yeah, me too. This matters."

Another police car came around the corner, lights flashing. A third followed. "Go home, people," the officer said.

"What are you gonna do, shoot us?" a man shouted. He raised his hands. "I'm unarmed. You gonna shoot me too?"

More people joined in shouting and chanting. The police got out of their cars, staying close together. None of them had helmets or riot shields, but they had their hands on their weapons.

"Stop it!" Annalisa cried over the rising voices. "This isn't how you remember someone who died."

Rascal cruised past the line of officers on his board, his phone held up to record the police as he rolled past. "Evening, officers. Smile for the camera. You're live on Rascal Streaming Video."

"Give me that phone," said the only woman officer in the group. "I don't care if you're a superhero or not."

"Freedom of the press," Rascal retorted, and scampered up a streetlight pole, using his powers to cling to it.

Wheels cantered over from where she'd been standing, Hothead at her shoulder. "Officers, I'm Wheels of the Neighborhood Watch. What seems to be the trouble?"

"This is an unlawful demonstration and you all need to go home now," said one of the officers.

"We ain't doin' nothin' wrong," someone shouted.

"Hands up, don't shoot," a strident female voice called. She repeated it like a chant and more people took it up.

Breezy pointed at the police. "They're callin' for backup," he said. "This is gonna get ugly quick."

Tendrils of smoke rose from the top of Hothead's scalp, suggesting he was a moment away from fully igniting. Annalisa realized that was the kind of event that could escalate a situation already on a hair trigger. "Wheels, get clear," she shouted over the chanting crowd. She dropped to the ground, wrapped her arms around Hothead, and took to the sky again just as his hair ignited. "Ow!" she yelped at the sudden flash of heat, even though it didn't really hurt so much as it surprised her. "Cut it out, Cole. You're going to burn my costume."

"Sorry," he gasped, trying not to struggle in her arms in case she lost her grip on him.

Sirens sounded in the distance. The three police officers were trying to look in every direction at once as the crowd of mourners transformed to protesters. "Breezy," Annalisa called. "Make a wind storm!"

Breezy nodded and raised his arms, calling upon the wind to do his bidding. He guided the rising breeze to blow across protesters and police alike. Dust swirled and sand peppered everyone, making them shriek and run for cover. The police ducked back into their cruisers as more cars approached, lights flashing and sirens blaring.

The crowd dispersed, thanks to Breezy's gale. Folks wiped dust from their eyes as they drifted away from the park in twos and threes. Annalisa watched to make sure nobody was hanging around to start any trouble, but it looked like Breezy's windstorm had ended the protest. He touched down amid the drifting dust cloud. Annalisa joined him, carefully setting Hothead down so he wouldn't flare up worse. "That was intense," she said, but faltered when she saw the miserable expression on Breezy's face. "What is it?"

"They're gonna hate us. Those folks. We sided against them."

Annalisa gasped. "We didn't side against anyone. I saw a situation getting bad and we defused it."

"Nobody got hurt," Hothead added. "That's got to be worth something, right?"

"You kids hold it right there," a police officer ordered as the approaching patrol cars came to a halt.

Breezy shook his head. "I ain't talkin' to five-oh tonight." Wind filled his cape and lifted him into the sky. Annalisa's heart went out to him. She understood how he felt, having used his powers to disperse the mourners. Those were his people. They were her people too. She glanced toward the light pole where Rascal had perched but he was gone. Wheels, too, had galloped away, leaving Hothead and Annalisa to face the police by themselves.

Be strong, she told herself. *You haven't done anything wrong.* She crossed her arms and stood still as the officers approached her and Cole.

"You're not supposed to be here," the officer said to Cole. Cole turned to look at Annalisa, stammering an incomprehensible non-answer.

"We can be here. It's a free country. We weren't doing anything wrong," Annalisa said.

The officer turned to her. She was tall, with her hair pulled back into a tight blonde ponytail. Her badge said *J. Olson.* "I don't see any supervillains, and that windstorm didn't come from a cloudless sky."

"We're allowed to appear in uniform." Annalisa had read enough of the Just Cause rules and regulations and committed them to memory that she felt she was treading on safe ground. "Superheroes do it all the time with Just Cause. Like when they go visit sick kids at the hospital."

Officer Olson frowned. "You're not in Just Cause, and you're juveniles. Using your powers against civilians is a crime."

"We weren't using our powers against anybody!" Annalisa said.

"What do you call what your friend did with the wind?"

"He was keeping people from getting hurt. Including you." Annalisa pointed at Officer Olson. "Those folks were just mourning, and then you showed up and escalated things."

"Be very careful, young lady," Officer Olson said. "You're going to get yourself into a lot of trouble."

"She's not doing anything wrong," Hothead said, his eyebrows smoldering. "None of us were."

Officer Olson's jaw tightened and Annalisa wondered if she was about to try to arrest them. She hadn't given any thought to what she should do if that happened. On the heels of that came the fear-not for her life, but for her future. The Hero Academy would probably reject her if she had a record. "Look, we're leaving, okay? We're sorry about any trouble. People are hurting and we're just trying to help. I know you are too."

"Stay away from any more protests, kids. You need to let us handle them. We can't look out for everyone. If you get in the way, you will be arrested just like anyone else. Is that clear?"

"Yes," said Cole. His entire head was smoking and Annalisa was afraid how the cop might react if it burst into full-on flames, as often happened when Cole got angry.

"Are we free to go?" she asked. Her mom had drilled that into her when she was younger. *Ask if it is all right to leave and then leave. Don't give the police a chance to detain you.* Cole's parents had probably never discussed that with him, but she knew Breezy's mom had. Brown kids and black kids had to learn about dealing safely with police more so than white kids did.

"Yes," said Olson. "I don't want to see you around here again. Go home, kids."

Cole grumbled under his breath that he would go to the damn park anytime he damn well pleased because it was a free damn country. Annalisa gathered him in her arms and flew away. Normally he complained about being carried like a sack of potatoes, but he seemed subdued. His temper was waning as quickly as it had flared.

"Hey," he said after a minute. "You need to go find Breezy. He's real upset."

"I don't know what to say to him," Annalisa said. "I'm afraid I'll just make things worse."

Cole smiled at her suddenly. "Yeah, maybe you will. But you might not. He likes you, Annalisa."

"I like him too."

"You better set me down. Don't worry, I'm not going to burn down the neighborhood or something. Besides, I kind of need to process what went down tonight. It's kind of, you know, uncomfortable being the white kid in that kind of situation."

"I don't think of you like that, Cole. You're just my teammate. And my friend."

"Every girl needs a Gay Best Friend." Cole had come out to her and the rest of the Neighborhood Watch at the beginning of the school year. It hadn't changed anything in the group dynamic, for which everyone had been grateful.

"You're such a dork." She dropped to the ground on a quiet neighborhood street. "You good to get home from here? I can fly you the rest of the way. I don't mind."

"I know you don't. No, I can walk. Go find Breezy, Annalisa."

She gave Cole a quick hug then flew off into the gathering darkness.

Chapter Six

Breezy where are u?
Breezy?

After a couple of minutes of pacing back and forth twenty feet above the ground, Annalisa decided Breezy wasn't going to respond to her texts or hadn't charged his phone. Her cape hung limp behind her as if it were an extension of her feelings. Her phone buzzed with a message and her heart leaped, hoping it was Breezy. Instead, it was Aighleigh and a wave of guilt washed over Annalisa as she realized her friend was probably worried sick about her.

Im ok, she sent back to Aighleigh. *Dropped off C n lookin for B no where he is?*

He's perching, Wheels replied. Her friend was always using words like *perching*. If it was anyone else, Annalisa would have thought they were showing off, but Aighleigh really had a vocabulary like that. She was the smartest person Annalisa had ever met. Someday, Annalisa was sure, Aighleigh would be in charge of Just Cause New York. And if she was lucky, she'd have Annalisa as her right-hand woman.

She had to Google *perching* and it told her *sit somewhere, especially high or narrow*.

She knew what that meant, and headed across town. There weren't any actual skyscrapers in

Loveland, but there was an office building that was six floors tall. If a superhero needed a place to brood, it was the best choice. Annalisa's dad had helped build that building, setting concrete forms and laying out glass-smooth pads of it to make the plaza around it. He was proud of his work and she was proud of him for it.

Then, thinking of her dad made her feel guilty all over again. Even though she was a superhero, her parents would still be worried sick about her. They hadn't texted or called her yet, which she supposed meant they trusted her to be safe. After she and the rest of the Neighborhood Watch had defeated their real supervillain, her parents had given her a little more freedom to be out without supervision. In return for that, she tried to be much more responsible about checking in with them. *Mom dad were all ok. Be home soon te amo <3<3<3.*

Te amo, Halcónita, her father texted back.

She spotted Breezy's cape flapping in the evening breeze like a flag at the corner of the office building. Her teammate sat with his legs dangling over the edge, elbows resting on knees and chin resting on upraised hands. She flew over to him. "Hey, Breezy."

He dashed one hand across his eyes and she knew she was supposed to pretend she hadn't seen it. For him to have been crying, he must have been terribly upset. "Hey." His voice was rough.

She sat beside him on the edge and put her arm around him. He stiffened for a moment but then relaxed and rested his head on her shoulder. She was about to speak when he sniffled and she froze. If he broke down right there beside her, she was half afraid she'd lose it too. He needed someone to be strong for him at that moment, and nobody was stronger than Annalisa. His shoulders shook for a few minutes and he kept wiping away angry, embarrassed tears. If he'd pulled away, filled his cape with wind, and flown off, Annalisa would have been hurt, but she would let him go, because it would be what he needed.

He stayed beside her, letting her hold one of his hands as she idly toyed with his dreadlocks with the other. At last, he took a deep, shuddering breath and said, "I betrayed everyone tonight."

"What do you mean? Of course you didn't!"

"Yeah, I did. I used my powers against them folks. Against civilians. Y'all ought to kick me off the team for that."

"Then they should kick me off too. I told you to do it."

"I didn't have to listen."

Annalisa snorted. "Yeah, how well has that worked for you so far?"

He chuckled, one brief lightning flash of amusement amid the dark storm clouds plaguing his heart. "I guess you're right."

"Things were getting out of hand, Breezy. More cops were showing up. People were yelling. Someone was going to get hurt. We stopped that from happening."

"Yeah, but folks ain't gonna think about that. They're gonna remember me blastin' wind. Far as they're concerned, I might as well have been wearin' a badge and a riot helmet."

Annalisa laid back on the roof, hands behind her head, kicking her feet over the edge. She stared up at the stars. "You know, one day when we're in Just Cause, we'll *have* badges. And we'll have to do stuff like we did tonight. It's like the words on the police cars. *Protect and serve.*"

Breezy lay back beside her, bundling his cape under his head like a pillow. "It's hard to see myself as a cop."

"Why?"

"All my life, all I ever heard about was that cops shoot black people. That we can't trust 'em because they don't trust us."

"There's black cops. Officer Bickle's black."

Breezy turned to look at her. "I bet he's had to deal with just as much racist bullshit as any other black man."

"But he's still a cop. Doesn't that mean he can rise above it? I know you, Breezy. I've known you since we were in preschool. You're a good person. You can rise above it, too." She smiled at him. "Literally."

He didn't smile back. "I just don't know, Annalisa. It's complicated. I'm havin' a tough time wrappin' my mind around it. I mean, I know not all cops are bad. They ain't all racists." His voice grew hard. "But the ones that are? They're the ones who shoot people in the back."

Annalisa took his hand. Her friend's heart was hurting, and she didn't know how to help him. Breezy wasn't normally a talkative young man, and for him to open up and share his feelings meant his mind was in turmoil. "All we can do is the best we can do," she said at last. "My dad says that. We know what's right and what's wrong, Breezy, and we've got powers. We can do something about it. We take our stand and we have to stick to it, no matter what. It's the best we can do."

"And it's all we can do, right?" At last, Breezy cracked a faint smile.

"We did the right thing tonight." Annalisa had never been so certain of anything in her life. "We kept things from getting worse. Nobody got hurt. Yeah, people are gonna be mad at us, but how many people are gonna be glad it went the way it did?"

"I dunno." He sighed. "I'm sure this ain't over yet, though."

"It is for us. For tonight," Annalisa said. "It's still a school night, and I need to head home pretty soon."

"Yeah, me too."

"You call your mom and tell her where you were? You know she's gonna worry about you."

"She worries 'bout all of us."

"Your mom's a good person, Breezy."

He snorted. "She still calls me *Bryson* half the time, even though she knows I hate it. She just does it to get a rise out of me."

"Does it work?" She nudged him in the ribs, making him jump and giggle.

"Hey! Yeah it does. And that don't mean you can start."

"You'll always be *Breezy* to me."

He made a breeze play around Annalisa's hair, but it was still too short to do more than flutter a little. "I wish you hadn't cut it. Now I can't blow it in your face."

She gasped and felt her face grow hot.

He turned away, realizing what he'd just said. "Aw, man . . ."

She squeezed his hand, careful not to hurt him. "I know what you meant." When he turned his head back to her, she leaned over and kissed him—not deeply or passionately, but a quick buss on the lips. She wouldn't have minded kissing him some more, especially in a deeper, more passionate way, but it was late, and she didn't want to be in trouble when she got home. "Is that better?"

He smiled. "Yeah. Yeah it is."

"Go home, Breezy. Hug your mom for me. I'll see you tomorrow in school." She floated off the rooftop, her cape fluttering in the breeze.

"Annalisa?"

She turned. "Yeah?"

"Thanks. I . . . I needed someone to talk to. Thanks for bein' here."

She flew back to him and kissed him once more. "You're welcome."

* * *

Thursday, May 7, 2020
Loveland, CO

It seemed to Annalisa the events of the candlelight vigil were the only thing anyone wanted to talk about in school the next morning. Students she barely knew at all came up to her, either to thank her for helping to support the cause, to blame her for breaking up the protest "Just when it was about to matter," or to thank her for supporting the police. The conflicting messages were making her head spin.

Breezy looked absolutely haunted when she saw him in the hall between classes. His eyes were shadowed and he yawned as if he hadn't slept a wink. "You okay?" she asked him.

He nodded. "Rough night. I'll be okay."

She went to the library for lunch instead of eating in the lunchroom. "Hello, Annalisa," said Torvald, the librarian. The slender, blonde-headed man was one of her few adult friends since she first came to the school, and was very supportive of her becoming a superhero. Although he was a real librarian, he was also an agent for the Parahuman Resources Administration, and he'd been posted to a long-term position in Loveland. Statistically, a town the size of Loveland might not have had any native parahumans because it didn't have a huge population base.

Instead, there were eight of them.

Besides · the five kids of the Neighborhood Watch, there had been identical triplets all with powers who called themselves the Culture Club. They moved on to New York with their mother two years earlier but for a while, there had been eight native parahumans in Loveland. Torvald and his partner Carson collected DNA samples from all eight kids and discovered that not a single one of them had the genetic marker common to the world's parahumans. Nobody knew what it meant, but Annalisa figured someone had maybe *made* her and her friends into parahumans. She didn't know who would have done such a thing, or why, but she intended to find out someday.

"Hi, Torvald. Can I eat in here today? It's really weird today."

He nodded. "Of course. I saw Rascal's video from last night. I imagine things are pretty . . . complicated for you right now."

She sighed. "I just don't know if we did the right thing. I mean, some people are saying we kept things peaceful—and I guess we did—but others are mad at us for it. It's like . . . they *wanted* there to be a riot." She opened her lunch box and unwrapped her *torta*. She liked when her dad made her lunches. As a construction worker, he needed a lot of calories to get through the day, and he preferred to make gigantic sandwiches that her mom affectionately called *fregaderos*, or kitchen-sinks. He usually made two at a time and would send half of one with Annalisa and stick the other half in the fridge for anyone who wanted it. Today's *fregadero* had leftover fajita meat and vegetables on a buttered bun, smeared with refried beans on the bottom half and guacamole on top.

"That looks delicious," Torvald said. "I'm going to tell Carson we should have tortas tonight." Carson was Torvald's husband as well as partner. He'd been a private chef for the girls of the Culture Club before they left, and now ran the kitchen at a fusion restaurant downtown. "I'm sorry you're having a tough day."

Annalisa swallowed a mouthful of her sandwich. "Why would people want to riot?" she asked. "I mean, they start fires and break windows, and then the police have to use tear gas and fire hoses." She'd seen videos of rioting in other cities when people were protesting, and that chaos scared her.

Torvald's face went solemn. "When people feel like they are powerless, they sometimes lash out. Have you ever heard the saying about cornered animals being the most dangerous?"

Annalisa nodded.

"People aren't animals in this case, but they can lash out when they're feeling cornered. When people feel as a group that they are being victimized, sometimes they choose violence over discourse. That's called *mob rules.*"

Annalisa opened her Coke and took a sip. "There's a chapter on riot control in *On Parahuman*

Combat. Sunstorm said *none of us is as dumb as all of us.* Is that like the same thing?"

Torvald chuckled. "I didn't know that was in there. Yes, it's the same idea. It's easier for a group to devolve into violent and antisocial behavior than it is for individuals, because it's easier for someone to misbehave when someone beside them is as well."

"So then you have a riot." She thought for a moment. "Have you ever been in one?"

"No, but I have been to protests before. It's not always easy being a gay man in America. Our rights are always being challenged. It's important to stand up for what you believe in, whether it's the right to marry whom you love, the right to be in charge of your own body, or the right not to be judged by your skin color."

"Do you think I should be protesting? I should have just let the riot happen?" Annalisa liked talking with Torvald, because he didn't treat her like a kid. He always challenged her with complicated concepts that she'd spend days thinking about afterward. She didn't know if it was part of his responsibilities as a PRA agent, but she suspected it was more because he wanted to help prepare her for a life as a superhero.

"I didn't say that, Annalisa. The problem with a protest that becomes a riot is people make poor decisions—decisions that hurt other people. I bet almost everyone in a protest is there to be heard, not to break windows or start fires or throw stones. Just like almost every police officer is there only to make sure people are safe instead of to use tear gas or batons or rubber bullets."

"But all those things happen!"

"It's like peer pressure. You remember those PSA videos about not doing drugs or drinking just because everyone else is doing it?"

"Yes." Annalisa finished her torta and washed the last bite down with more Coke.

"Peer pressure is the same thing as mob rules when it comes to riots. Protesters do things they wouldn't normally do because *everyone else is doing them.* Police do things *they* wouldn't normally do for the same reasons."

"So what am I supposed to do? How do I know what's right?" She sighed. "I'm supposed to be a superhero. I'm supposed to do the right thing."

Torvald smiled. "You're fourteen years old, Annalisa. You've barely had any life experiences to draw upon yet. Even so, sometimes there is no right answer to a problem like this. My advice to you is to follow your heart. You know deep down what's wrong and what's right. You're a principled, moral person. Trust yourself."

The bell rang to signify the end of lunch. Annalisa gathered the remains of her lunch and wiped down the table where she'd eaten with a cleaner wipe Torvald handed her. "Thanks, Torvald. Give Carson a hug for me."

"I will. Annalisa . . ." He paused as she turned back to look at him. "After this school year, Carson and I are being reassigned. With the Culture Club already gone and the five of you leaving for the Hero Academy, there's no need for us to remain here. We'll be working in the Los Angeles PRA offices."

Annalisa gasped. She hadn't ever considered the possibility that Torvald just wouldn't be around anymore. "Los Angeles? Not Denver? You won't be around at all?"

"I'm afraid not. I'll make sure you have our contact information in case you need to reach us for something, but . . . Darn it, Annalisa, I'm going to miss you."

She wanted to hug him, but it was in school, and even though he was gay, he was still an adult and she was only fourteen. She didn't want to get him in trouble, especially so close to the end of the year and the end of his career in the school. "I'll miss you too, Torvald."

He gave her a bright smile that almost looked forced. "You better get on to class or Ms. Shelby is going to be very put out."

Chapter Seven

Annalisa barely had time to sit in her seat in Geometry before a student assistant from the office entered the room with a note. Ms. Shelby read it then said, "Annalisa, please go to the office."

Guilt immediately made her stomach clench, even though Annalisa didn't think she'd done anything to warrant a trip to the principal. Maybe someone who had seen her flying through the hall had reported her. *Technically* that was against school policy, but hardly serious enough to pulled out of class. "What is it? I didn't do anything."

Ms. Shelby smiled. "I'm sure you didn't, but they're asking for you. Your homework will be posted on Campusnet. Email me if you have any questions about what I'm covering today."

Annalisa grimaced. She was already fuzzy on calculating surface area and volume and missing an hour of instruction wasn't going to help her get any less fuzzy. Nevertheless, she shouldered her backpack and followed the student assistant into the hall. "What's going on?"

He shrugged. "I dunno. The SRO is there. Maybe they want to talk to you about last night."

"I didn't do anything wrong."

"That's not what I heard." The student assistant didn't sound like he was accusing her of anything so she kept her anger in check. He opened the office door and the other kids of the Neighborhood Watch looked up as Annalisa walked past the secretary's desk. The secretary, a pleasant young woman named Egret, looked up from her computer and smiled before getting back to work.

Breezy looked glum. Aighleigh was trying to cheer him up without much apparent success. Cole spun a pencil through his fingers, tongue poking out from the corner of his mouth. Doing a simple, repetitive physical task helped him keep his emotions in check, which was imperative when to lose control would likely mean igniting the office. Vinnie leaned back in his chair, thumbing through social media posts on his phone, looking as bored as ever.

"Hail, hail, the gang's all here," Annalisa said. "What's this all about?"

Principal Harstein was the kind of woman who seemed to fill a room despite her short stature. She was a former Phys Ed teacher and wrestling coach, and she looked like she could take the School Resource Officer two falls out of three. She'd been generally supportive of the kids of the Neighborhood Watch, but from the serious expression on her face, Annalisa didn't think she'd had them all pulled out of class to congratulate them on another job well-done. "My office will be a little cramped with all of us," she said. "Egret, we'll use the meeting room."

"Okay, Diane. Do you need anything?"

Harstein shook her head. "No, I don't think this should take very long." She led the kids to a meeting room in the back offices. "Please sit down, everyone."

Annalisa and Vinnie sat and slid their chairs apart to make room for Aighleigh's wheelchair between them. Breezy and Cole sat across from them. The SRO sat at the opposite end from Principal Harstein. Annalisa glanced at him but she couldn't read anything on his face. His arms were crossed and his mouth made a thin, expressionless line.

"Well, here we all are," Harstein said. "Three weeks left in the school year and then the five of you are off to the Hero Academy. Are you all looking forward to it?"

The Neighborhood Watch kids muttered their acquiescence.

Harstein nodded. "Of course. You're about to embark upon what may be the greatest adventure of your lives. I'm a bit envious. I always wanted to be a superhero. Unfortunately, I don't have any powers, so I had to go out and get a real job instead."

Annalisa bristled. Who was she to say being a superhero wasn't a *real job*? She happened to know that Just Cause team members made a pretty good living. They started at something called a GS-10 pay scale and it went up from there. She didn't know what that meant from a practical standpoint, but it was more money than she'd ever imagined.

Harstein continued on, blithely unaware of Annalisa's slow burn. "Before we begin, Officer Potter has something for you kids. Go ahead, Trevor."

The SRO opened a folder on the table and withdrew a piece of paper. He cleared his throat. "This is a letter from the Mayor. *To the Neighborhood Watch. I want to officially express my gratitude for your efforts to help keep the peace. Loveland is a safer place thanks to you.* And she signed it." He put the paper back in the folder and closed it.

Harstein smiled at the kids around the table. "A copy of this letter will go into each of your files. It's an official commendation. You should all be very proud of that."

For a moment, Annalisa felt proud of herself and her team. They'd *earned* that commendation through hard work and rising above all odds. On the heels of that pride came a deep-seated suspicion. They hadn't been pulled from class and brought to the principal's office just so they could get an official pat on the back. She glanced at Vinnie, who was by far the sharpest when it came to recognizing trouble from authority figures. His arms were crossed and his lips slightly pursed in a barely-disguised expression of contempt. He'd felt it, too.

Harstein cleared her throat. "Now, the real reason I brought the five of you here is to talk about what happened last night."

Annalisa opened her mouth to retort, but Aighleigh was faster. "You mean *what happened last night off campus outside of school hours*, am I right?"

Harstein's cheeks turned pink. "Yes, I'm aware that is outside of immediate school jurisdiction, but the fact remains that the five of you are associated with Malley Middle School as much as if you were athletes. Your behavior outside of school reflects on this school for good or for bad, and I want to stress that point with the five of you."

"Did we do something wrong?" Aighleigh said. "Because it looked to me like we *helped keep the peace*."

"Yeah, that's what the Mayor said in her letter," Cole added.

"There are numerous reports that the five of you used your powers."

Breezy crossed his arms. "It was just me. Nobody else did nothin'."

Annalisa couldn't let him take the blame upon himself. "He did it because I asked him to. The crowd was getting really angry at the cops, and the cops looked like they were getting angry too. You aren't a parahuman and you probably haven't studied them as much as I have. Breezy's powers are nonlethal. It was safe for him to do what he did. It stopped things from getting worse."

"We're not disputing that," said Officer Potter. "Honestly, I'm glad it didn't get any worse. I've got a lot of friends on the force and the last thing anybody needs in this town is a riot. It's bad enough that somebody's dead."

"Because cops shot him in the back!" Breezy leaped to his feet.

"Sit down, Bryson," Harstein said. "You are out of line."

Breezy stood quivering, his fists clenched at his sides. Annalisa could feel the fury radiating off him, like he was Hothead about to ignite. How could the truth be out of line?

"Breezy, please," Annalisa said. "Please sit down." She glanced back at Potter and was horrified to see his hand had strayed beneath the table, toward his hip.

Breezy's hands opened. He wouldn't look at anyone except Annalisa. "Sorry," he whispered, and sat back at the table.

The SRO's hand came back up to rest on the table beside the folder with the Mayor's commendation in it.

"Let me be clear on this," Harstein said. "You're not in trouble here at the school. It's three weeks until the end of the year and I'm not looking to pass out suspensions. However, I can't have the five of you causing trouble here in the school by politicizing yourselves outside of school. Do you understand what that means?"

"You don't want us to go to any more vigils," Aighleigh said. "In case they turn into riots and we have to be heroes and stop them. Got it."

"You're minors," Potter said. "Underage. Maybe someday you'll be superheroes and have law enforcement powers, but right now, you're putting yourselves and civilians at risk."

Annalisa's ire rose. What did he mean, *maybe*? She would be a superhero no matter what. If Just Cause wouldn't have her, she'd be a Champion. If she couldn't be a Champion, she'd be an independent hero, or even a vigilante. She wasn't a parahuman; she'd been *given* her powers, and she had sworn a long time ago to use that gift to help whomever she could.

"So we're just supposed to sit by and let things fall apart?" Vinnie asked. "When we can stop it without hurting anyone? Give us some credit here. We're pretty good at what we do. We've been practicing for years."

Harstein sighed. "I can't stop you from doing whatever you choose to do off this campus, but I want the five of you to think very carefully about your choices. You need to do the right thing and let the police and community leaders handle any tensions that arise. I know you want to help, but you don't have the training for it. All it takes is one misuse of one of your powers for someone to get hurt or worse. If that happens, the consequences will be far more serious than any of you can imagine."

"Yeah, I guess we could wind up dead," Annalisa said. "Shot in the back."

"That will be quite enough, Annalisa." Harstein's expression turned thunderous at Annalisa's cutting remark. "You're a smart group of kids, but you are still kids, and while you are students at this school, you are my responsibility. I won't have the five of you causing any trouble among the student body the rest of this school year. I've been lax in enforcing the no-powers rules because none of you have abused them during your years here. That ends now." She crossed her arms, making it clear she would not be negotiating anything. "I'm implementing a zero-tolerance policy until the end of this year, and I will inform all staff to be vigilant and to enforce that policy *rigorously*. Any breach of this trust will result in a suspension. I hope you will take steps to ensure that does not happen. Do I make myself clear?"

"Yes, Ms. Harstein," Annalisa said, and the rest of the Neighborhood Watch echoed her. Her pulse throbbed in her temples. It was their right to peaceably assemble. That had been covered in the Constitution unit in Social Studies. It was the First Amendment. The important one. "We won't use our powers."

The principal nodded. "Then I believe we're done here for now. I'm not your enemy, kids. I have an entire school of students to watch over, including the five of you. I want you to enjoy your last three weeks here at Malley, and to do so safely."

All things being equal, Annalisa reflected as she left the office with the rest of her team, she'd rather have been suspended.

Chapter Eight

"So that was pretty terrible," Aighleigh said as she cracked open a Coke from the minifridge and handed it to Vinnie. "*Don't color outside the lines.*"

"I have a problem with authority," Vinnie added.

"Just one? You're so tolerant," Cole said.

Vinnie snorted with a mouthful of Coke and spluttered helplessly as the bubbles went up his nose.

"So what do we do about it?" Breezy asked. He'd been quiet the rest of the afternoon, clearly deep in thought following their meeting with Harstein.

"There's going to be a protest tonight," Vinnie said, wiping his nose. "It's already all over local feeds. I think there are people coming from out of town to join it."

Aighleigh frowned. "That's a problem."

"Why?" Annalisa asked.

"Say a bunch of people from Denver show up. They don't know us, don't know our town, don't know our people. They could start a whole lot more trouble and then fade away back to Denver again. We don't want Loveland to become a battleground."

"It's that whole *mob rules* thing Torvald was telling me about today," Annalisa said. "The more people are in a group, the easier it is to cause trouble because the group reinforces their behavior."

"Oooh, fancy big words," Vinnie said. "Someone's been *reading.*"

"You ought to try it sometime," Aighleigh said.

"Hey, I'm passing English."

"Barely. I've seen your grades."

"I think we should go tonight," Annalisa said. "But, you know, undercover. Like, in disguise."

Aighleigh did a quick wheelie in her chair. "I'm not really good at the whole incognito thing. People may look away from a kid in a wheelchair a lot of the time, but it stands out more than someone who's walking around on two feet." She raised a hand to forestall any protests from the others. "Don't worry, I'll stay here and coordinate everything. I'll get dragonflies all over the place and keep an eye on the crowd. If there's trouble, I'll try to direct you guys."

"Do you need help with that?" Annalisa asked.

"I wouldn't say no to a second pair of eyes and hands. It's tough to keep more than two dragonflies in the air at one time."

"I'll stay," Cole said. "If someone pisses me off, well, everyone will know it's the kid with the flaming head."

Vinnie grimaced. "Um . . . I was gonna stay too."

"No," Aighleigh said. "You need to be there in person. Boots on the ground. You're like the social media guru. You need to be livestreaming it, Vinnie. Get it out there for your Ragers to share."

Vinnie shrugged. "Yeah, that makes sense. I got a lot of followers, and this is the kind of thing that goes viral."

"So that's it then," Breezy said. "Me, Vinnie, and Annalisa makes three. My question is what are we supposed to do? I mean, do we walk around? Hold up signs and chant like everyone else?"

"We stay on the edges," Annalisa said. "If there's gonna be any trouble, it'll be there, where the protesters and the police are closest together."

"What if someone in the back starts breakin' windows or throwin' Molotov cocktails?" Breezy asked.

Vinnie laughed. "Are you for real?"

"Hey, it could happen. We've all seen it online."

"We just need to watch for it is all," Annalisa said. "If somebody starts something, we need to shut it down."

Breezy smiled. "Hey, they don't start none, there won't be none."

* * *

Annalisa had to beg to go to the protest. She had a long discussion with her parents at the dinner table. "It's only going to lead to violence, *Halcónita*," her father said. "I know you're bulletproof and super-strong and you can fly, but I still worry."

"Papi, what if I stay home and somebody gets hurt —or worse—because I wasn't there to save them?"

"People get hurt at protests," her mom said. "Police might use fire hoses or tear gas. You still have to breathe, Annalisa."

"I'll be careful, Mamá. You're gonna have to get used to it sooner or later, because you know I'm gonna be on Just Cause someday and then I'll be fighting supervillains and aliens."

Her mother bowed her head and Annalisa knew she was praying.

"Be careful, *Halcónita*. Look out for your friends. I would go myself, but . . ." Her father wouldn't meet her gaze. "*Me temo que.*"

Annalisa squeezed her father's hand, carefully so not to hurt him. "It's okay to be afraid, Papi. We're just going to keep an eye on things, and to keep people from getting hurt.

"We love you, Annalisa," her mother said. "And we're very proud of you."

"*Te amo,*" Annalisa said, and ran to her room to prepare.

She discussed what to wear and what to bring with Vinnie and Breezy, and they all agreed that costumes needed to be left at home. Even though it was hot, she dressed in jeans and a lightweight dark hoodie. She tied a bandana around her neck and tucked it into the front of her hoodie so she could pull it up over her nose and mouth to make an improvised air filter and to help disguise her identity if needed. If she used her powers, it was kind of pointless, but she felt like maybe it would be important to be masked. She had a twisting in her gut that she got whenever she knew she was about to do something she shouldn't.

Aighleigh researched a list on the internet of things to take to a protest and posted it on the Neighborhood Watch app. Annalisa checked over the list and decided nothing would be a problem. She dumped out her school backpack and put some emergency supplies into it instead—water bottles, the box of vinyl gloves she'd swiped from the kitchen, some granola bars, and a portable phone charger.

The backpack went over her shoulders. Her costume stayed where it was, hanging on the hook on her bathroom door. She paused to look at it, wondering if maybe she should take it. She could even put it on underneath her clothes, although that was a lot more uncomfortable than it looked in the comics. No, they'd agreed to be incognito and she would adhere to that decision.

She opened her window, flew out, and carefully shut it with the handle her father had installed for her.

The sun was just touching the mountains to the west as Annalisa flew over the trees toward the office building where she planned to meet Breezy and Vinnie. It felt weird to be flying without wearing her costume. She was used to her cape flapping behind her. Instead, the hood of her hoodie tugged at her throat in a way that wasn't quite uncomfortable, but she didn't think she would get used to it anytime soon. The water bottles in her pack sloshed around, which was also annoying. By the time she touched down on the office building's roof, she felt out-of-sorts all around. She was pretty sure it was a combination of the minor irritations and the one big stressful event the three young heroes were about to attend.

Breezy smiled at her, and his easy grin made her feel better almost immediately. Like her, he was wearing a hoodie, although he'd supplemented his with a Colorado Eagles baseball cap. Annalisa knew they were a hockey team, but the closest she'd ever been to a game was when she'd met the members of the Culture Club atop the rink one time. "You a hockey fan now?" she asked.

He shrugged. "My mom had it. I dunno where she got it."

"Isn't it uncomfortable to wear on your dreads?"

"It stretches ok. It ain't bad." He looked her up and down. "You look all . . . normal. I like you better in your costume."

She smiled at him. "I like me better in it too. This feels like cheating." She looked around. "Where's Vinnie?"

With a whoop, Vinnie jumped off the stairwell roof, flipping his board in midair before landing on the nearby air conditioning unit. He did a grind along one of the pipes until he lost his balance and went sprawling on the gravel of the rooftop.

"Oh, there he is," Annalisa said as she and Breezy hurried over to their friend. "Are you okay?"

Vinnie gave her a thumbs up and then started picking bits of gravel off his hands. "I meant to do that. I always finish a big ollie with a slam. The chicks dig it."

Annalisa snorted. "Well, I don't dig it."

"You're not a chick."

It was Breezy's turn to snort. "I disagree."

"No, Annalisa's one of us. You know, part of the team."

"Keep digging that hole deeper," Annalisa suggested.

"That makes her, you know, *better* than just a chick."

Breezy rolled his eyes but Annalisa nodded. "Okay, I guess I can accept that. It's still sexist."

"You know I don't mean anything by it," Vinnie said.

"That doesn't make it okay," Annalisa said.

"Yeah," Breezy said. "How'd you like it if someone called Aighleigh a *chick*?"

Vinnie paused, appearing to really think it over. "Yeah, okay. You're right. I'm sorry, Annalisa. And I'm not just saying that because you can throw me off this building." Vinnie pirouetted on his board's back wheels. "So are we gonna go do this or what?"

"Yeah, let's go. I'm worried that something might happen." Annalisa rose into the air. A moment later, Breezy filled his cape with wind and it lifted him from the rooftop.

Vinnie looked up at them with a devious grin. He reached into his own backpack and withdrew his Rascal mask. Using his powers, he adhered it to his face. "I'm positive something will."

"Hey, I thought we agreed we were going to be, you know, incognito," Annalisa called as Vinnie vaulted over the edge of the building and rode his skateboard down the vertical face, using his powers to keep himself firmly glued to the wall through the wheels of his board. When he'd first discovered his adhesion abilities, he practiced until he could extend them as far as his skateboard wheels.

"I'm grinding down the side of a building," Vinnie said. "Anybody looking is gonna know it's me. And they're gonna know it's you because, you know, *flying*."

Annalisa and Breezy flew down alongside their skateboarding friend. "I mean after we get there."

Vinnie skidded across a window, reversing his stance from right-foot forward to left. "After we get there, the mask will come off. There's a story to be told tonight, and Rascal's Ragers are gonna get it firsthand." He found a long, decorative vertical piping and straddled it, grinding down it on the board trucks. It would have been a world record if anyone had been tracking it. "Race you guys there."

Chapter Nine

At first, the protest seemed like it was going to go smoothly, the way Annalisa had hoped. There were a lot of people—not just black and brown faces, but a lot of white folks had joined in, holding protest signs, chanting, and singing along with their brothers and sisters. It felt good to see people coming together for a common cause, even if that cause had been triggered by Dominic Ortega's death.

Breezy stayed with Annalisa as they wandered the edges of the protest. Vinnie split from them as soon as they arrived at the park, promising to stay in touch via the Neighborhood Watch app if he needed them or they needed him. He ran a long charger cord from his phone to the battery in his pocket and began reporting on what he saw. Annalisa knew the more he broadcast, the more people would tune into and share his livestream. Vinnie wasn't particularly suave or politic, but he had a strong journalistic sense and if there was a story to be found, he tended to be in the middle of it.

"There are a lot of people here from out of town," Breezy said in Annalisa's ear so she could hear him over the chanting group nearby.

"Why do you say that?"

"See them?" He nodded toward the group. "There ain't that many black folks in Loveland, and I ain't never seen any of them before."

"You think they're from Denver?"

Breezy shrugged. "Could be from anywhere. I guess it's okay. The more the merrier, right?"

Annalisa glanced toward the police. A couple of dozen officers stood off to one side. None of them had their riot gear on, which she thought was probably for the best. They were watching the protesters but not engaging with any of them. A few protesters were speaking with officers, and it seemed like the conversation was at least cordial, if not friendly. Annalisa spotted her friends, officers Bickle and Velez among the officers. They normally worked the day shift but she figured they might have been called in for extra duty. Bickle towered over his fellow officers, a good six inches taller than the next tallest. Velez had her arms crossed, her lips pressed tight, and stood in front of Bickle as if she were his bodyguard.

She wondered if she should go over and say hello, but they were working, and technically, so was she. She'd have to check in with them later.

A buzz of excitement ran through the crowd and Annalisa was sorely tempted to fly up so she could get a better look at what was transpiring. She needn't have bothered, for she got an alert on her phone from Aighleigh. *Mayor just arrived.* As if to remind Annalisa that she and Breezy weren't completely on their own, one of the dragonfly drones dropped down from the sky to circle her a couple of times before heading back up into the darkness again. Aighleigh would have all of them recording, just in case something happened and they needed video evidence beyond Vinnie's livestream to back it up.

"Come on, I want to hear what she has to say." Annalisa took Breezy's hand.

"The Mayor's a lady?" he asked.

"How do you not know that? We met her two years ago."

"Ain't there been an election since then?"

"Yeah, she won again."

"So she's good?"

"I guess." Annalisa pushed through the crowd, not above using her strength occasionally to force her way between the press of people. She spotted Vinnie standing at the very edge of the crowd, holding his phone up among a forest of other arms doing the same.

The Mayor—Annalisa remembered her name was Babcock—was a tall white woman with her dark hair gathered in a bun. She smiled at the protesters as she emerged from her car, which had been escorted by a pair of motorcycle police. "Hello, hello everyone," Babcock said, putting on her best politician's smile.

"Mayor, where's the body cam footage?" someone shouted. Other people shouted similar questions until Babcock raised her hands for peace.

"I'm sorry to say there's no body cam footage. The City hasn't had the budget for them, but I can assure you I am bringing it up at the very next Council meeting."

"What about the dashcams?" A black woman called. "You haven't shared more than a few seconds of it."

Annalisa involuntarily squeezed Breezy's hand, making him jump and wince. "Sorry, B," she said, and leaned in to kiss his cheek. The video she'd shot might be tremendously important.

"There's nothing conclusive in the dash video," Babcock said.

"Then why can't we see it?" A woman called. "What are you hiding?"

The Mayor raised her hands. "Please, let's all remember that a man is dead—"

"He's dead because white cops shot him!" someone called. "Shot him in the back!"

A police officer took Mayor Babcock's elbow as if to encourage her to return to her car but she shook herself free. "We're investigating the incident. I assure you, nobody wants a peaceful resolution to this more than I do."

"Why ain't those cops in jail?" another voice yelled. "Murderers are s'posed to go to jail!"

"We are still investigating—"

The crowd shouted the Mayor down. Annalisa wished they would all shut up and let the woman speak, but it was like Torvald had said. The mob was ruling. "Hands up, don't shoot! *Hands up, don't shoot!*" Someone had a bullhorn and was leading the chant. It was spreading through the crowd like wildfire through bone-dry mountain pine trees, until even Annalisa found herself struggling to resist joining in.

The urge to participate was powerful, and she couldn't help but remember some of her own experiences with racism. She'd been asked to leave a store when she was just walking through the mall and went in to look at a t-shirt she'd liked. She remembered store employees following her dad around one time when they'd gone to buy some tools for his work. She'd even had someone yell something at her from a passing car that sounded suspiciously like *Go back to Mexico*. Why *shouldn't* she join in with the chanting with her fist in the air?

Then she remembered her police friends, Bickle and Velez. One was black, one was brown. They were good people. They liked their jobs, and they'd always been respectful to her even though she was just a kid. Other officers had been polite and friendly too, whether they were white or not. Just because they were wearing uniforms didn't make them bad people.

It made them targets, though, and insults and heckles were being directed toward the officers. A subtle feeling made its way through the crowd as the shouts transformed from righteously angry to openly hostile. The police felt it too, for they moved in groups of four to back away from the lines and return to their cruisers, where they retrieved helmets and plastic shields. In the space of a few minutes, the two-dozen police officers were fully geared up for a potential riot.

"This is getting ugly," Annalisa said to Breezy, having to shout to make herself heard over the chanting and the invective. "You think we ought to leave?"

Breezy shook his head. He had a sharp cast to his jawline beneath the shadow of his hoodie. "They ain't wrong," he said. "The cops shot Ortega in the back. That's murder, Annalisa. And you saw it yourself. They were gonna cover it up."

"We'll figure something out."

Breezy's laugh was short and sharp. "We? We're just a bunch of kids. We ain't figuring out *shit*."

Something crashed nearby, and people screamed as several police officers surged into the crowd. A moment later and three of them had taken down a heavyset black man with a shaved head. "I didn't do nothin'!" he screamed as an officer knelt on his back, wrestling the man's arms behind him.

"Let him go!" a strident-voiced woman shouted. "You're hurting him!"

"Get back!" An officer bawled, his eyes wide and his nightstick raised.

Annalisa started forward, not knowing what she was going to do but knowing she had to do something. A hand grabbed her from behind and she whirled, fists clenched, ready to do some damage.

"Annalisa! It's me!" Vinnie yelled. His mask rode atop his head like a hat and his pale face was smudged with dirt, plain even in the darkness. The intensity of his expression made her pause. "You can't stop this. None of us can."

The mayor's police escort rushed her back into her car as the tone of the crowd changed from chanting to angry shouts. The woman with the strident voice screamed as two officers took her down, pulling her arms behind her back and applying handcuffs.

"Everyone clear this area," an officer ordered, his voice blasting from the speaker on the roof of his car. "We will deploy crowd control measures if you do not disperse immediately. You will not get a second warning."

"That means gas, Annalisa," Vinnie said. "We've got to go."

"Let 'em try it," said Breezy. "I'll blow it all back in their faces."

"Breezy, no!" Annalisa knew he was still smarting about using his powers to disperse the previous protest and wanted to make amends. "This isn't the way."

Breezy's mouth dropped open. "No, you can't take their side, Annalisa. You ain't one of them, you're one of us."

"It's not *us* versus *them*, Breezy!"

Vinnie grabbed her arm again. "It is tonight, Capitána." He pulled his mask from the top of his head and jammed it onto his face. He vaulted over a park bench, reaching for his skateboard as he ran toward a sidewalk where he could use it.

A police officer, perhaps surprised by Vinnie's leering demonic mask, struck the boy with his baton. Vinnie went down like he'd been shot.

"*Vinnie!*" Annalisa screamed, and launched herself into the air, all pretenses at staying incognito forgotten. She shouldered aside the officer, who was reaching for his handcuffs. He tumbled back, shouting in pain and surprise at Annalisa's impact. He crashed against some of his fellows, who were hurrying over to provide backup, and the entire group went sprawling.

Annalisa didn't know how badly Vinnie was hurt. He wasn't moving. Maybe he'd been knocked out. She knew you weren't supposed to move someone who was injured, but she had to get him to a place of safety. Even unconscious, his mask still stubbornly stuck to his face thanks to his powers. She gathered him up in her arms, keeping herself between Vinnie and the approaching officers.

"Freeze!" someone shouted. "Set him down and put your hands in the air."

Annalisa glanced back over her shoulder and saw a cop, helmet on his head, hand on the butt of his pistol. His eyes were wide and he looked terrified and furious at the same time.

"No."

She took to the sky with Vinnie clutched in her arms.

"Hold it right there!" A cop shouted.

A concentrated blast of wind passed by Annalisa, strong enough even to make her short hair whip. "No!" Breezy shouted as he directed winds toward the police. "Leave them alone!"

Without his cape, Breezy couldn't fly, and that made him an easy target. An officer who was out of the line of fire crouched raised his hands, a boxy device with a yellow tip clutched in them. Breezy jerked suddenly and fell. Cops swarmed over him. Almost at the same time, thick clouds of stinging white smoke filled the air as several tear gas grenades sprayed their noxious chemicals.

Annalisa hovered, not knowing what to do. Tears poured down her face, but not from the gas so much as from impotent fury. She couldn't help everyone. Breezy was face-down on the ground, his hands zip-tied behind him. He wasn't moving. If he was dead . . .

She made her decision as the tear gas reached for her. She couldn't help Breezy. She couldn't fight the entire police force. No, she *could* have—and she could have won—but that wouldn't help anyone. Vinnie was hurt, though, and she could help him.

She flew toward the hospital.

Chapter Ten

Annalisa burst into the hospital emergency room and shouted she needed help, just like in a movie. The response from the hospital staff was efficient but far less dramatic than a movie. They took Vinnie from her right away and wouldn't let her accompany him into triage. The security guard, a heavyset Hispanic man, stood nearby, his arms crossed and full of suspicion as Annalisa passed Vinnie's information to the receptionist—at least, what information she knew. No, she didn't know his parents' names. No, she didn't have their phone numbers, but she was pretty sure her mom did. She knew his dad was an ex-pro skateboarder who'd been a big X-Games athlete twenty years earlier, and his mom was a tattoo artist. She texted her mom and got the phone numbers in return.

Are you OK? Are your friends OK? her mom texted.

vinnie got hurt i brought him to the hospital, she replied. *plz call his folks for me. im ok. tell u l8r what happend.*

She asked again if she could come in to see Vinnie but the receptionist was apologetic. "I'm afraid not, sweetie. You're not family. I will see if they will tell me how he's doing, but it's only been a few minutes."

"You get mixed up in that riot?" The security guard asked. "I heard that there were superheroes there."

Annalisa's ire rose but she forced herself to keep it in check. Her friends needed her to stay clear-headed. She needed to find out what had happened to Breezy, but she couldn't leave Vinnie before his parents arrived. "We were there. They used tear gas on us."

"That's rough," said the guard. "I'm sorry. We're not all that way." He tapped his badge. "My mom and Dominic Ortega's mom go to the same church. I might have been down there if I wasn't working." His suspicion seemed to melt away as he smiled at her. "I think you kids do good work."

"Thanks," Annalisa said, and suddenly felt like breaking down into tears. The guard must have noticed the wave of emotion and discreetly stepped away to give her some privacy.

She pulled out her phone and Facetimed Aighleigh, from whom she had about a zillion unread messages.

"Oh my God, Annalisa, are you okay?" Aighleigh's worried face filled Annalisa's phone screen, with Cole pressing in so he could see too. His eyebrows were smoldering.

Annalisa turned down her phone volume to keep the chat more private. "I'm fine. I'm at the hospital with Vinnie. A cop hit him."

"We saw," Aighleigh said. "And they tased Breezy. I got it recorded, but it's dark and jumpy because I was trying to keep the dragonfly from getting smashed."

Annalisa's heart skipped a beat. "I saw him fall. I was afraid they'd shot him. I . . . I didn't know what to do. I flew away with Vinnie."

"You did the right thing," Aighleigh said. "If you'd tried to get to Breezy, they might have tased you too. We've never tested your powers for that. You might be vulnerable to it."

"But I might have saved him."

"Annalisa, think about it for a second. I know you could fly holding both him and Vinnie, but neither one very well. If you'd gone down there, you might have gotten hurt . . . or worse. Then all three of you could be . . . worse."

Annalisa felt tears roll down her cheeks. "I abandoned him."

"Think about what Sunstorm said in *On Parahuman Combat.*" *On Parahuman Combat* was the definitive book on the subject, written by a former Just Cause commander and Hero Academy Dean of Students. Torvald had given Annalisa a signed copy two years ago and she'd probably read through it a dozen times since then until it was smudged and the cover was creased like an old textbook. She'd lent it to Aighleigh, who had wrapped a textbook cover around it before returning it. "There's no shame in retreating to regroup, because some fights can't be won."

"So where is Breezy now? Did they arrest him?"

Aighleigh smiled. "Nope. When the police deployed the tear gas, they fell back and in the confusion, they left him on the ground and a couple of the protesters grabbed him. They carried him away from the park. I followed them with a dragonfly. The Urgent Care down the block was taking in tear gas victims and the protesters brought him there. He was uncomfortable but he could move and talk and everything." She chuckled. "He wanted to know which cracker son of a bitch had tased him."

Annalisa brayed a surprised laugh and then covered her mouth.

An ambulance braked to a halt outside the E.R. and the paramedics unloaded a half dozen coughing people with reddened, puffy eyes. "Tear gas," one of paramedics said to the security guard as they started bringing the people inside. "There's going to be more behind us."

Annalisa lowered her voice. "Aighleigh, what should I do? Stay here or go to Breezy?"

Aighleigh considered it for a moment. "Vinnie's mom is on her way to the hospital now. I, uh, I'm tracking her phone." She glanced over at Cole's open-mouthed surprise. "What? I'd rather know where she is then get . . . you know, surprised." She blushed suddenly and for a moment, Annalisa wanted to ask what she meant before it dawned upon her. *Surprised* . . . like being *interrupted*. Like kissing, or . . .

"Yeah, I know." Annalisa sighed. "Okay, please tell her I'm sorry I didn't stay but I've got to go check in with Breezy. You didn't call his mom yet, did you?"

"No, I was about to when you called."

"I'll call her." Annalisa swallowed hard. That was a conversation she wasn't looking forward to having. "Let me know what they say about Vinnie."

"Will do. Be careful, Annalisa."

Annalisa slipped out of the waiting room and into the parking lot. The evening air had a hint of coolness about it and she was glad she'd worn her hoodie. Being bulletproof didn't make her any less cold.

"Hey, that's her!" someone said. "That's La Capitána!"

Annalisa turned to see a young Hispanic couple clapping and smiling at her. They both had red eyes but hadn't gone into the E.R. yet. A black man behind them looked solemnly at her and slowly raised one fist into the air. She felt a weird sense of pride and accomplishment even though she didn't think she'd really done anything. Instead, she nodded back at the trio, and gripping her phone, flew straight up into the darkness.

Once she got some altitude, she spun around once to get her bearings. Flashing lights amid an ugly, pale cloud marked the park, where everything went wrong. Aighleigh had thoughtfully dropped a pin on Google Maps to show where to find Breezy. Annalisa oriented herself and flew in that direction. She knew she couldn't put it off any longer, and called Breezy's mom.

Mrs. Cooper answered on the second ring. "Annalisa, is that you?"

Annalisa's tongue froze in her mouth. Breezy's mom knew her number? And on the heels of that thought, of course she would—all the Neighborhood Watch kids' parents probably had all their numbers. Superheroes or not, they were still minors, and parents would want to have every chance to get hold of one of them in an emergency. "Y-yes, Mrs. Cooper."

"Please, call me *Amanda*, Annalisa. Is Breezy with you? I've been trying to reach him and he's not answering his phone. If he left it uncharged again, I will tan his hide."

"No, uh, Amanda."

"Do you know where he is?"

Annalisa felt worse than she ever had in her life. Delivering bad news was horrible. Mrs. Cooper was going to hate her forever, and probably forbid Breezy from spending any more time with her. Maybe even make them break up . . .

if a couple was what the two of them actually were. "Mrs.—uh, Amanda . . . Breezy's at th-the clinic by the park." Tears raced down Annalisa's cheeks. It felt like she was cutting out her own heart with a blunt knife.

Amanda Cooper said nothing, but the sharp intake of her breath over the phone sent Annalisa into full-on bawling.

"I'm s-so sorry! And it's—it's all my fault. We were going to leave, and th-then Vinnie got hit, and I went to help him, and I didn't see Breezy in time, and they sh . . ." She couldn't get the last part out at all.

"Did they shoot him? *Did they shoot my son?*"

"J-just with a t-taser. Oh God, I'm so sorry."

"Is he hurt? Are you with him now?"

"Aighleigh said he's not hurt." Annalisa paused to wipe her eyes that were stinging from the combination of tears and the wind of her headlong flight. "I'm almost there."

"I'm leaving the house now, Annalisa. I'll be there shortly. Stay with my son until I get there." Mrs. Cooper hung up the phone. Annalisa felt like she'd managed to break everyone's trust. Sooner or later she'd have to deal with her parents as well.

Then her shame would be complete.

The clinic was packed full of people who'd breathed in the tear gas. They were coughing and crying. Annalisa landed behind the building, then walked around to the front. Normally on a Thursday night, there might only be one or two cars in the lot. Instead, it was packed and a crowd waited outside, breathing the untainted air and trying to get their symptoms under control. Annalisa kept her hood up and walked into the building. She'd learned her lesson at the hospital and knew the best thing would be to keep herself covered.

The overworked staffers were running back and forth, working on treating those suffering the worst symptoms. Annalisa waited for an opportune moment, and then slipped into the hallway off of which branched a half dozen exam rooms. She heard Breezy before she saw him.

He was arguing with a nurse. "Look, man, I'm fine, okay? Let me go and use this room for one of them folks who actually needs it."

"I'm sorry, son, I can't do that," said the tall young man with tattoos decorating his forearms. "You're clearly underage, and you won't tell us your name so we can contact a parent or guardian."

Breezy's eyes widened as he saw Annalisa looking in the doorway at him. "His name's Bryson Cooper," Annalisa said. "And I'm here to collect him. His mom is on the way."

The nurse turned and Annalisa saw he had another tattoo at the base of his throat. He looked her up and down. "You know this young man?"

Annalisa nodded. Her throat had closed up and she knew if she said anything at all, she'd start crying again. She felt completely drained. This had to work. She didn't think she could take one more defeat.

"Yeah," Breezy said. "She's my girl . . ." Had he been about to say *girlfriend*? Annalisa's eyes spilled over once again.

"All right," said the nurse. "Kid, you're right about one thing. I do need this room. Go wait outside for your mom, but please don't leave. Last thing we need is liability for a missing kid. We're not set up to deal with a riot aftermath here." He thrust Breezy's backpack at him. "Keep those bandages dry and clean for the next day. And for the love of God, stay away from any more riots." He hurried Breezy into the hall and pointed to an older Hispanic man hunched over, moaning and rubbing his eyes. "Sir? Right in here, please."

Annalisa grabbed hold of Breezy there in the hallway, threw her arms around his neck, and kissed him. His arms encircled her waist as he kissed her back, and for a long moment she forgot everything else.

Chapter Eleven

After what felt like an eternity spent melded together in the hallway, as people flowed around them to either side, Annalisa and Breezy broke their kiss. Both were breathless and Annalisa's heart raced like she'd been in a hard workout. Her cheeks were wet and she realized she was still crying. Breezy wiped away her tears, which didn't help her stop.

"Hey . . ." he began, uncertain and awkward. "Hey, uh, Annalisa. Don't cry. I'm okay, see?"

"You scared the hell out of me." The words came out more sharply than she'd intended, and she winced as Breezy recoiled a little. "I'm sorry. Don't be mad. I was afraid the police had shot you. I mean, really shot you. Vinnie was already down and hurt and I didn't know what to do."

"Annalisa, it's okay, really. I ain't mad at you. And I'm okay. They just tased my ass. I'm sore, and I got a couple band-aids on where the dart things stuck into me, but I'll be fine. Is my mom really on her way here?"

She nodded.

"Aw, shee-it. I'm gonna be on punishment so bad." He grimaced. "Is Vinnie okay?"

"I don't know. I think so. They wouldn't tell me anything at the hospital because I'm not family."

Breezy took her hand. "We're all family. They don't know nothin' about us." He led her out of the clinic. She let him. "I was stupid. I shouldn'ta let them get so close to me back there when I didn't have my cape, but I got so mad when they started breakin' out the gas. I mean, look at these people. They were just there to protest police violence, and the cops did exactly what the folks were there to protest." He sighed. "I should probably see if Wheels can make a suit to protect me. I ain't bulletproof, and it looks like I ain't taser-proof neither."

Annalisa's phone buzzed. She pulled it out to read a text message from Aighleigh. "Vinnie's got a concussion but he's okay otherwise. Guess he's on the shelf for a bit."

Breezy sighed. "I probably am too. I mean, I don't think mom'll let me do any superhero stuff for awhile. On account of me gettin' tased and all."

Annalisa kissed his cheek. "Battle scars. I hear chicks like them."

"Ain't no chicks around here. Just powerful and independent ladies." Breezy smiled.

Annalisa realized he had a scratch on his cheek that he hadn't had earlier in the day. She wondered if he'd gotten it when he fell after being tased and her good cheer vanished as quickly as it had arisen. She bowed her head. "I could have lost you tonight. That cop could have reached for his pistol instead of his taser." Her hands shook and she clenched them under her arms. "I don't even w-want to think about that."

"Annalisa, we ain't just gonna be superheroes *someday*. We're already heroes. We do it because other folks can't. And if that means puttin' ourselves on the front line, then that's what we gotta do. We said that when we started the Neighborhood Watch all them years back. It ain't changed."

"You sound like Cole."

"Cole's one smart motherf—"

"*Bryson!*"

Breezy actually cringed at the sound of his given name. Amanda Cooper swept in like a safety zeroed in on a receiver, but instead of the play ending with Breezy flat on his back with cartoon stars spinning around his head, she wrapped him in her arms and held him like she might never let go.

Annalisa suddenly felt like the third, fifth, and forty-seventh wheel all at the same time. She glanced around, wondering if she was brave enough to simply fly away in front of all those people. They'd know who she was the moment she took to the sky, and they'd call to her. Maybe they'd cheer for her. Maybe they'd curse her for failing to stop the police. Or for not helping them sooner. She didn't think she could face that kind of attention at the moment, and she pulled her hood a little further over her face and hunched a bit so she'd be a bit harder to see.

"Annalisa . . ." Amanda Cooper's voice made her freeze in her tracks.

She slowly turned, hands in her pockets. "Y-yeah?"

"Thank you for calling me and for coming to check on Breezy." Ms. Cooper's words were warm but her tone was frosty, and Annalisa felt the chills running up and down her back.

"You're welcome."

"We'll talk about this later, after I've had time to process it all. For now, I'm taking my son and going home."

Breezy looked helpless, shrugged, and mouthed *sorry* at Annalisa. She nodded. When

Breezy's mom made up her mind, no mere parahuman was going to change it, no matter how strong she might be.

"I'll—I'll follow you." The words came out in a rush. Annalisa nearly surprised herself with her vehement desire to protect Breezy. She'd come so close to losing him, and to be honest with herself, she was afraid of letting him out of her sight. "Make sure you get home okay."

"That won't be necessary."

"But . . . but . . ." Annalisa couldn't figure out how to put her feelings into words. Maybe if she had a day to watch cheesy romance movies she might get some ideas. She was tired and wired all at the same time. The combination of the two had her brain broadcasting a steady low-res static hum, like a speaker with a bad wire. She couldn't think. "I'll text you," she said to Breezy at last.

His face fell. "I lost my phone." His eyes widened immediately as it registered what he'd just said.

Amanda Cooper's tone grew even darker. "Then I guess you won't be texting anybody for a while, young man. That's good, because I'll have plenty of chores to keep you busy. Come along, Bryson."

Breezy grimaced. "I'll see you at school tomorrow."

"Yeah . . . you too." Annalisa couldn't take it any longer, and leaped into the sky, letting the darkness wrap around her like a blanket.

She flew home.

Her parents were sitting on the back porch, drinking beers and watching their cell phones, when Annalisa dropped to the yard with a thud.

"Annalisa!" her mom cried, and ran over to embrace her. "I was so worried about you, *bebita.*"

"Mamá, don't worry. I'm b-bulletproof." Suddenly, Annalisa was crying hard into her mom's shoulder. Her father came over and put his arms around both of them.

"Shhh . . ." Annalisa's mom stroked her short hair. "*Está bien, hija.*"

"No, Mamá, it's *not* fine. Everything fell apart tonight." Annalisa buried her face against her mother.

"Not everything, *Halcónita.*" Her father squeezed her and her mom together. "You're alive. Your friends are alive. There's much to be grateful for."

"B-but the police . . . they hurt Breezy and Vinnie. They used *tear gas*, Papi. Tear gas!" Annalisa's ire rose as she remembered the pale cloud spreading out across the park. "We weren't doing anything. Just standing around and, like, chanting and singing. Being peaceful."

"Sometimes police overreact," her father said. "Sometimes the protesters do too. I was your age in Los Angeles when the riots happened there. It was a scary time to be in South Central."

Annalisa wiped her eyes. Her father hadn't spoken about that before. He picked up his beer and took a long, thoughtful sip before bowing his head enough to keep his eyes in shadow.

"I didn't know that, Papi. What did you do?"

He shrugged. "I couldn't do anything. I was just a kid. I'm not a superhero like you, *hija.* I did what most of the kids in my neighborhood did. We kept our heads down so the police and National Guard wouldn't use them for target practice. We stayed away from the trouble areas." He sighed. "I wish you would stay away from them too."

"The people need me, Papi. They need to know someone is on their side."

"But you're going to be a superhero. Law and order."

"There's law and order, but there's also right and wrong," Annalisa said. "What the cops did, shooting Mr. Ortega in the back like that, that was wrong. Hitting Vinnie with a nightstick and tasing Breezy, that was wrong too."

"You can't go in there thinking that the police are your enemy, Annalisa," her mother said. "If you fight them, that makes you the criminal. The *bad guy*. That's not who you are. You're a hero. It's in your blood, although God knows where you got that blood from."

Annalisa frowned. Her parents didn't often bring up the fact that neither of them were carriers of the Musashi parahuman genetic structure, and nobody had been able to explain why Annalisa had powers. One thing she knew about her blood was that it was calling her to action. She couldn't sit by and let the violence in the streets play itself out without trying to stop it. Her fists didn't have to be her first response. Adding to the violence wouldn't do anything except escalate it. One way or another, she'd find a way to bring peace.

And she would find a way to bring justice to Dominic Ortega's family, because they deserved that closure. She had a video with what she thought was some pretty damning conversation from the cops who had shot him. That was what Aighleigh called *leverage*. It meant that the Neighborhood Watch had some negotiating power with representatives of the city. They might be kids, but they were also superheroes, and that carried a certain amount of cachet with city officials. Maybe they could broker some kind of peace between the protesters and the police.

Annalisa looked up at her parents. "Mamá, Papi, I won't fight the police, but I've got to stop them from hurting protesters, just like I've got to stop the protesters who are throwing things and trying to hurt the police too. I can't pick just one side or the other."

"That's a very mature way of looking at the problem, Annalisa," her mom said. "You might not realize it, but you're a symbol. Your costume is a symbol. It means hope for a lot of people. They see a strong, Hispanic girl doing the right thing, and that inspires them to do the right thing too."

"Even the police?" Annalisa felt doubtful. She'd seen the fear and anger on the officers' faces behind their riot helmets.

"You're a superhero, *Halcónita*. You *are* what it means to *protect and serve*." Her father finished his beer and walked over to drop the bottle into the recycle bin. "Once they stop being afraid, they'll see that."

"But how do I stop them from being afraid?"

Her father sat down beside her. "If I knew that, I wouldn't be working in construction."

Annalisa laid her head on his shoulder. "I'm glad you are, Papi. I like sitting on top of your buildings and looking out over the city."

He put his arm around her. "*Soy el padre más afortunado del mundo.*"

"You're the luckiest dad in the whole world, Papi?"

"The whole world, *Halcónita*."

Annalisa smiled. He might have thought he was the luckiest father in the world, but she was even luckier to have him. She yawned.

"Bedtime for you, young lady," said her mother. "Tomorrow's a school day."

"Aw, really? Since when do superheroes have bedtimes, anyway?"

"Since I said so."

"Can I go to Mr. Ortega's funeral?" Aighleigh had posted on the Neighborhood Watch app that the service was tomorrow, followed by a march.

"If I tell you no, I suspect you'll find a way to get there anyway. I'll call and excuse you for it," her mother said. "On one condition."

"What's that?"

"You wear your costume. No more skulking around in hoodies. Be a superhero for the people, Annalisa."

Chapter Twelve

Friday, May 8, 2020
Loveland, CO

Annalisa awoke to the smell of frying tortillas and her stomach twisting in hunger. She hadn't gotten around to eating dinner the night before, and she was a growing superhero. She dashed across the hall to use the bathroom, wash her face, and brush her teeth. A few minutes later and she floated into the kitchen, leaning back and tying her shoes.

"Watch where you're going, Annalisa," her mom said as she shredded *queso blanco* onto a plate. "You're going to knock something over."

"No I won't." Annalisa pirouetted in midair. "I'm a great flyer." She rubbed her belly. "That smells really good, Papi."

Her father scooped a couple generous spoonfuls of the fried tortilla triangles onto a plate, added a scoop of scrambled eggs mixed with leftover chicken fajitas, then spooned red chile sauce over it. Her mom sprinkled the shredded cheese on top and handed the plate to Annalisa. "Neither of us remembered feeding you last night," her father said. "So I got up early to make you a big breakfast."

Breakfast was Annalisa's favorite meal of the day, and chilaquiles was one of her favorite breakfasts. "It's not the weekend," she said. "Am I staying home? Are you?"

"No and no," said her mom. "But we can't let you starve either."

Annalisa nodded, her mouth full of food. "Thank you," she managed between bites.

"Have you heard from Vinnie or Breezy?" her father asked.

Annalisa felt a twinge of guilt. She hadn't even thought about her injured teammates in the few minutes she'd been awake. What kind of friend was she? She pulled out her phone to check it for updates. Aighleigh had sent a lengthy message that took five separate sections to deliver. Annalisa skimmed through it and got the gist of it. Vinnie was home with a mild concussion and orders to stay in bed and no superheroing at the moment. There was a brief message from him as well. *Thx for bein my hero. I owe U.* At first, she was upset Breezy hadn't messaged her, then she remembered he'd lost his phone at some point between the protest, being tased, and being taken to the clinic. She dashed off a quick text to Aighleigh to see if maybe her friend had a spare phone for Breezy.

"Vinnie's home," Annalisa said. "He's got a concussion. I guess he won't be in school today. Um, Breezy lost his phone so I don't know how he's doing. I can let you know later when I see him."

"All right." Her mom set her costume on the edge of the table, wrapped up neatly in the cape. "I washed this for you. At least you'll look your best at the funeral today."

Her father set his plate on the sink. "I've got to go. Concrete truck arrives in an hour and we've got forms to finish setting." He poured some coffee into his travel mug, sprinkled it with the cinnamon-sugar blend he liked, and slapped the lid on top.

The doorbell rang, making Annalisa jump.

"It's seven o'clock in the morning," Annalisa's mom grumbled as she stepped into her shoes. "Are your friends picking you up or something?"

"No, Mamá."

Her mom stalked from the kitchen into the front room and a moment later she called, "Annalisa, Omar, can you please come out here?"

Annalisa looked at her dad and then the two of them left the kitchen together.

Officers Bickle and Velez were standing just inside the front door. Bickle smiled when he saw Annalisa but Velez looked as serious as ever. "Good morning, Mr. and Mrs. Torres, and Annalisa," Velez said. "We're sorry to disturb your breakfast. May we ask Annalisa some questions?"

Annalisa's mom glanced at her, eyes narrowed. "What about?"

"We've spoken to several witnesses who placed her at the park last night in the midst of the protest and we'd like to ask her about that," Bickle said. "Is that all right?"

"I suppose so."

Bickle smiled at Annalisa. "Don't worry, we just need to get your statement is all, Annalisa." He pulled out his phone. "I'll be recording our conversation to make sure I don't miss anything."

Annalisa pulled out her own phone. "I'll be recording too." She smiled.

Bickle nodded but Velez frowned. They asked her to tell her story about what had happened at the protest the night before. She was as truthful as she could be, recounting her experience and trying not to leave anything out. "Did you see the incidents involving Vincent Terasco and Bryson Cooper?"

Annalisa nodded. "Vinnie was trying to leave and an officer . . . I guess, maybe Vinnie startled him. He hit Vinnie with his nightstick thing. Breezy—I mean Bryson—saw it too and he tried to protect Vinnie and that's when he, uh, got tased." She got teary-eyed all over again at the memory. "I c-couldn't help him because I already had Vinnie, so I took him to the hospital."

Her mom put a soothing hand on Annalisa's back, lending her motherly strength to her daughter.

"Where did you go after you left the hospital?" Velez asked.

"I went to go see Breezy. Someone brought him to the clinic after you, uh, the police used tear gas."

"And how long did you stay there?" Velez made a note on her pad.

"I don't know. Until Breezy's mom picked him up."

"What is this about?" Annalisa's mom asked suddenly. "Annalisa has school this morning and my husband and I have work."

"I'm sorry, ma'am," Bickle said, and Annalisa thought he probably meant it. He was a genuinely nice person. "There was an . . . incident overnight at the local police station, and due to its nature, it was likely perpetrated by someone with parahuman abilities."

"You think my daughter did it, whatever it was?" Annalisa's mom's voice got that frigid tone which made Annalisa glad it wasn't directed at her. "She came home right after she left the clinic and she was here the rest of the night."

"What was the incident?" Annalisa asked.

Bickle glanced at Velez, who nodded. He opened a folder and withdrew a picture that had been laser-printed on copy paper. It was a photo of the police station, but someone had spray-painted MURDERERS in large, black block letters across the front of the building. Annalisa immediately understood why they thought a parahuman must have done it. For a normal person, it would have taken a long time using ladders or a crane, and that kind of effort wouldn't have gone unnoticed.

A flying or wall-walking parahuman could have done it with a half-dozen cans of spray paint and a few uninterrupted minutes. There probably weren't cameras pointing at the second floor of the police station. She nearly said *oh, shit* out loud, but her mom would have grounded her and she remembered not to just in time.

"Well, I'm sorry, officers, but you'll have to go look somewhere else. Annalisa didn't do that. You have my word."

Bickle nodded. "Of course. We're just following up on any potential leads. We're sorry to have bothered you, Mr. and Mrs. Torres. Annalisa, it's good to see you." He paused. "I hope you don't think less of us after last night."

"I guess not." Annalisa sighed. The truth was that she really didn't know *what* to think.

The two officers went to the door. Bickle let himself out but Velez paused in the doorway. "Oh, Mrs. Torres, I did have one more question for you. Has Annalisa ever sneaked out without your permission?"

Annalisa's ears grew hot and her pulse thudded in her ears. Velez was supposed to be her *friend! How dare she?*

Annalisa's mom cleared her throat in the way that Annalisa knew meant she was seething inside. "Officer, Annalisa has never left this house without my permission. Now if you will excuse us, we have jobs and school to get ready for."

Velez nodded. "Of course. Have a safe day." She closed the door behind her. Annalisa watched through the front window as the two officers got back into their cruiser and it pulled away from the curb with Bickle behind the wheel. He and Velez were having a fairly animated discussion when they left and Annalisa was pretty sure it was about her.

"The nerve of that woman," Annalisa's mom grumbled. "*Esa mierda puta.*"

Annalisa's eyes widened. She'd never heard her mom curse before. "I didn't do it, Mamá. I swear."

Her mother's eyes flashed with anger. "Of course you didn't do it. We raised you better than that. And they have the nerve to come in here and suggest to me that you did."

"Mamá . . . I need to tell you something. I've, uh, I've sneaked out before. I just open my window and fly out so you don't hear. I never did anything bad, though. I just go out to do, you know, superhero things."

Annalisa's dad put his hand on her shoulder. "You're not as stealthy as you think you are, *Halcónita.* Every time you raise that window, one of us hears it."

Annalisa's mouth dropped open. "But . . . but why didn't you ever say anything to me? Why didn't you . . . ground me or something? Not that I want you to," she added quickly.

"Because we raised you right, *hija*," said her mom. "I know you're not going out and getting into trouble. That's not who you are. You're our daughter, and you're a superhero. You're the one stopping other people from getting into trouble. You'd do that even if you didn't have your powers, because even when you were a toddler, nothing made you angrier than to see injustice."

"We trust you," said her father. "But would you please check in with us when you leave? Even though you're bulletproof and super-strong, we worry. And we love you, Annalisa."

Annalisa felt her eyes fill with tears. "Oh, you guys are the best." She flew across the living room to hug her father and then whirled to embrace her mom.

"Annalisa, do you know who might have done the graffiti on the police station?" her mother asked. "You don't think it's any of the other Neighborhood Watch kids, do you?"

"No." Annalisa wiped her eyes. She'd been thinking about it and she couldn't see how anyone she knew could have done it. "Only Breezy or Vinnie would have been able to get up there and mark it without anyone seeing, and they were both in the hospital last night. Oh!" An idea occurred to her, and she didn't like where it took her.

"What is it?" her father asked.

"I just thought of something. It's probably nothing, Papi, but I need to check it out." She looked at the clock on the fireplace lintel. "I need to go or I'm going to be late to school."

Her father grimaced as he, too, noticed the time. "Ah, hell. I'm going to be late, too."

"I could fly you to work, Papi. You'll miss all the traffic."

"What, you mean carry me through the air like a sack of groceries?"

"I carry people all the time. It's easy."

He laughed. "How would that look to the guys on the crew, having you fly me to work like a parapowered chauffeur? No, *Halcónita*. I'll just fight through traffic. You've got bigger problems than getting your old man to work."

"Okay. I would, though, just so you know." Annalisa's parents had never once flown with her and she'd never actually offered before. It was one of those things she'd just never thought about. "Mamá, can I still go to Mr. Ortega's funeral? I think it's important. And I want to be there in case . . ."

She didn't finish her statement, but she didn't have to say it. *In case things go wrong.*

"Yes, *hija*. I'll call in to excuse you."

"Thanks, Mamá. Love you guys." Annalisa grabbed her backpack, with her costume carefully packed inside, and ran out the door.

Chapter Thirteen

Annalisa could have flown to school. Her parents allowed her to do it from time to time, so long as she landed before she reached school property and walked afterward. She decided to take the regular school bus instead, as she was looking forward to a few minutes of down time where she could check in with her friends and teammates. She made it to the bus stop just as the school bus rolled to a halt. She filed on board along with the other dozen kids in her neighborhood who rode it to Malley Middle School.

There were a lot more whispered conversations on the bus than typically occurred, and Annalisa caught a lot of veiled looks pointed in her direction. When she happened to meet someone's gaze, they would invariably turn away, or look down at their phones, or at their seatmates. She didn't think they were angry at her, but the word was out about the previous night's protest, and most of the school probably already knew Breezy and Vinnie had been hurt.

A student whose name she couldn't remember turned around in his seat to look at her. "What's up?" she asked him.

He held up his phone, showing a picture of the police station with the MURDERERS graffiti painted across it. "You do this?"

She shook her head. "I don't know who did it, but it wasn't me."

He considered her answer and then shrugged. "Whoever did it oughtta get a medal for calling it like it is."

"Hey, cops aren't murderers, Dez," said Ty Smith from across the aisle.

"Tell that to Dominic Ortega," said Dez.

Annalisa sighed. She'd hoped to be able to text Aighleigh during her bus ride but it appeared she had other things to handle first. She got up from her seat and stood in the aisle so she could address the two boys. "Dez, not all cops are murderers."

Dez frowned and a look of triumph crossed Ty's face, but it went away when Annalisa pointed at him. "But two of them might be, because they killed Dominic Ortega. The world isn't black and white. Or brown and white. It's . . . complicated."

A loud cab-calling whistle came from the bus driver. "Sit down or you're walkin'," she called.

"Sorry," Annalisa said and returned to her seat.

Someone started clapping, then someone else joined in and a moment later, the entire bus was applauding. Even Dez and Ty, who a moment ago had looked like maybe they'd have preferred to solve their differences with a good old-fashioned fistfight, were clapping for Annalisa.

She wished she could melt through the floor of the bus, or turn invisible. What had she done to warrant such adulation? All she did was keep two boys from starting a fight in the back of the bus. The applause died down in a minute and she buried her head in her phone, trying to tune out the rest of the world.

Is Rascal comin 2 school? she texted to Aighleigh.

No. Neither is Breezy. Dr.'s orders.

Did U have n xtra phone for B?

Yes. Cole dropped it off. His mom has to set it up on the account. He said he'll message you later.

Annalisa smiled to know she and Breezy wouldn't be incommunicado for much longer. Then her smile faded as she considered how to word her next text.

Did U see the grafiti on the police statn?

Yes, came the immediate reply. *I was going to ask if you knew anything about it.*

Not until cops came to my house this AM. I didnt do it.

I didn't think you did. It's not your modus operandi.

Annalisa snorted aloud. There was Aighleigh flashing her vocabulary again. *IDK what that means.*

It's not the way you do things. Are you getting off the bus or what? I'm getting old sitting out here waiting for you.

Annalisa looked up and realized the bus had stopped in front of the school and most of the kids were already drifting across the courtyard toward the entrance. She grabbed her backpack and hurried to the door. "Sorry!" she said to the driver and skipped down the steps.

Aighleigh and Cole were waiting for her. "Some night, huh?"

Aighleigh spun her chair around and wheeled across the cement. "Yeah. I wish I could have been there to help out."

"You guys did help. I needed more eyes than I had, and you gave me that."

"But maybe Breezy and Vinnie wouldn't be hurt," Cole said. "I hate feeling like I can't do anything to help."

"Aighleigh, I need to ask you something important. That graffiti on the police station. Could a drone do it? Like the ones you fly?" Annalisa kept her voice low so no other passing students would overhear.

"Are you asking me if I did it?" Aighleigh's voice didn't sound rancorous, but Annalisa felt like she was tap dancing on a landmine. She didn't want to hurt their friendship. Aighleigh was the only female friend she had.

"No, of course not! I know you better than that. But the police think it was someone with parahuman powers, and if that's the case, then it's somebody new—somebody we don't know. I'm asking if someone who knew how to make stuff could make a drone into a flying paint sprayer."

Aighleigh shrugged. "Sure, I guess. It's not really that difficult. If you had a good modeling program, you could get it to draw precise enough to make letters. Have you ever seen the videos of synchronized drone art? Like when they're tricked out with LEDs and they move in patterns and form shapes? That's the same kind of thing." She frowned and pulled out a notebook and pen. "Hmmm. I have an idea. Would you push me to class?"

Cole snorted. "Really?"

"Sorry, I left my legs in my other pants." Aighleigh patted her knee. "And I need to draw."

"What's your idea?" Annalisa asked.

"So the problem with using a drone as a paint sprayer is that the updraft from the propellers would screw up the spray, and then your motors would fill with paint gunk and pretty soon you'd have an expensive paperweight." She made a quick sketch of a four-motor drone. "You'd need a super-long nozzle like *this* . . ." She drew the extension. "So it would be clear from the updraft. You'd need a larger compressed air tank to drive the spray, and you'd need a tank of paint too . . ." She drew the tanks on the underside of the drone. "Then you'd just need to program it to follow the right pattern and *voila* . . ." She traced some spray coming out of the nozzle and then froze as she realized what she'd drawn looked like.

Cole and Annalisa both giggled. "And that's how it is, is it?" Annalisa asked.

"That's quite a . . . unit." Cole barely got the sentence out before dissolving into laughter.

"Screw you guys," Aighleigh said, and tore the page out of her notebook. She didn't crumple it up or throw it away, Annalisa noted. Instead, she folded it and tucked it into one of the pouches on her wheelchair. "Anyway, if someone actually took the time to build one of these, they'd still have to program it. And it would be super noisy while it was working on the outside of the building. Also, and I just thought of this, the letters would look like a font. You know, they'd be, like, regular. Look at the picture." Aighleigh showed the other two the image of the police headquarters with the graffiti on it. "Someone sprayed that on by hand. It looks like spray-paint handwriting, not typing."

Annalisa frowned. "Then the police are right. It's someone with powers."

"Someone we don't know," Aighleigh added. They looked around, as if considering that any of the students in the courtyard might suddenly announce him- or herself as the culprit. "It could be anyone."

"It's probably someone from out of town," Aighleigh said. "I can't believe there would be yet another unknown native parahuman in this town. The odds against it are astronomical."

"Astro . . . You think it's an alien, maybe? Like the Hind?" Cole asked with a half smile, suggesting he was joking.

"Like anybody could miss a giant flying centaur-lion thing floating around the police station with a box of spray cans." Aighleigh chuckled. "No, it's probably one of the protesters who came in to support the locals. That makes the most sense."

Annalisa frowned. "Whoever it was just made things worse. The police aren't happy being called out like that. It's going to make things scarier at the march today. Are you guys going?"

Cole studied his shoes while Aighleigh cleared her throat in an uncomfortable way. "Well, um, it's like this. My dad kind of said I'm not supposed to go. He's worried about violence between the protesters and police, and my quadropede isn't set up for running yet. If I get caught in the middle of some trouble I can't get away quick, and, well, he's worried about it."

Annalisa nodded. She understood Aighleigh's reticence. "It's okay, Wheels. I feel better knowing you've got my back with your dragonflies anyway." She turned to look at Cole, whose ears had grown red to the point where she wondered if the tips might ignite like candle flames. "How about you, Hothead?"

He grimaced as if he'd eaten a bad taco and mumbled something under his breath.

"What?" Annalisa put her hands on his shoulders. She wasn't exactly using her strength to turn him to face her, but she wasn't exactly *not* using it, either.

He sighed. "Look, I'm scared, okay?"

Annalisa realized his hands were shaking and he had tears in his eyes. "Cole?"

"I'm just . . . I'm not as brave as you are, Annalisa. I'm not bulletproof. I'm not super-strong. All I can do is catch on fire, and then I'm a danger to everyone else. People throw cigarettes out car windows all the time and start forest fires. What if I started a fire in town? W-what if someone died because of it? What if someone shoots *me* because I'm on fire?"

"I wouldn't let them." Annalisa wrapped her arms around Cole. He sniffled against her shoulder but the hitching of his shoulders stopped after a moment.

"I'm sorry, Annalisa," he whispered. "I can't go. I'm sorry. I just can't. Not after what happened to Vinnie and Breezy."

The first bell rang and kids in the courtyard hurried for the doors into the school.

"It's okay to be scared, Cole. I'm scared too."

"But you're bulletproof."

"I'm not afraid of getting hurt that way. I'm afraid of other people getting hurt, or worse. I'm afraid someone is going to do something stupid and then a lot of people will get hurt today. I've got to go. Maybe I can keep things civil."

"You're really the best of us, Annalisa," Aighleigh said.

"I'm just trying to do the right thing. I know you guys are, too."

The second bell rang. "Crap, we're late," Cole said.

"I'll be fine," Aighleigh said. "I'll just play the wheelchair card. What are they going to do, give the crippled girl detention for being late?"

"What am I supposed to do, play the gay card?" Cole retorted.

Annalisa shrugged. "If the fabulous shoes fit . . ."

Chapter Fourteen

Annalisa kept one eye on the clock and one hand on her backpack for the first two periods that morning. She didn't pay attention in the least to the lessons, but at least she wasn't the only one. With only a couple weeks remaining in the school year, a great many students were daydreaming about summer vacation, sleeping in until noon, and playing video games past midnight.

After an interminable wait, the bell dismissing them from second period rang and Annalisa had to remember to keep her feet on the ground as she hurried out of the classroom. She weaved through the congested hallway, shouldering past younger students. "Hey, Annalisa!" someone called. She turned to look and saw a boy from her grade smiling at her. "My mom said she saw you save someone's life last night at the riot. Good job."

Annalisa smiled back. She didn't do the superheroics for the accolades, but nevertheless it was nice to be recognized. She ducked into the restroom and went to the far stall, oversized to accommodate *differently-abled* kids—although Aighleigh would have snorted at that and called it *handicapped*. "And don't ever let me hear you calling me *handi-capable*, either," she'd said once, up in arms about it at a sleepover. "I'm handicapped, because I can't run. But that doesn't mean I still can't kick your ass, Annalisa." She'd grinned. "I'll just build a robot to do it for me." And both girls had laughed.

That had been a good time, when they were younger and life didn't seem as serious.

Unlike now, Annalisa reflected as she stripped out of her clothes, when police were shooting unarmed civilians in the back and trying to cover it up.

On the other side of the door, girls ran in and out of the bathroom, using the toilets, touching up their makeup, texting, taking selfies. Annalisa ignored them as she changed. They would leave her alone in a few minutes.

She pulled her deodorant from her backpack and gave her pits a good going-over. It wouldn't do to stink or show stains on a day where solemnity was paramount. Her mother had freshly laundered her costume, and it sparkled even in the dull fluorescent bulbs of the restroom. She stepped into the bodysuit's feet and pulled the suit up over her hips, then slid her arms into the sleeves. The zipper was in the back, hidden beneath her cape when she wore it. It would have been awkward to reach if the suit didn't stretch enough for her to kind of spin it around her so she could get it closed up properly. She had to readjust her boobs once it was fully-closed, because her sports bra never stayed in the right place once her costume was on. It was a problem she hadn't had when she was younger.

The bell rang and the bathroom emptied as girls headed to their classes, leaving Annalisa in silence.

She slid her boots onto her feet and wiggled her toes, feeling them touching at the tips. She'd need larger boots pretty soon. Her body ached and she knew she was going through a growth spurt. She ignored the pain as much as she could—she hoped when she was done growing that she'd be tall and statuesque, the way a superhero *ought* to be.

Her cape went on over her shoulders, catching on the snaps on her costume. She didn't want to lose her cape ever in a fight, but if someone grabbed hold of it, they'd be left holding a piece of cloth, not her. She pulled a black armband over her right bicep. Her mom and dad had explained it would show she was in mourning.

At last, she pulled on her gloves and shoved her clothes into her backpack. She stepped out of the stall and checked herself in the mirror. She saw herself in the reflection, but more importantly she saw a superhero. A symbol. Resplendent in her green, white, and red, she smiled at herself. She looked good.

She peeked out the door into the hall beyond. It was quiet and abandoned. She smiled and slipped out, heading for the nearest exit. As she rounded a corner she nearly ran into the school resource officer, who stood with his back to her, checking something on his phone. She froze and immediately lifted herself a couple inches off the floor lest an errant footstep give herself away. All he had to do was turn slightly and he'd see her move out of the corner of his eye. She glanced around, trying to figure out where she could go.

Further down the hall, Torvald emerged from the library on whatever business might cause the librarian to emerge from his natural habitat. He saw Annalisa and his eyes widened. She shook her head at him, silently pleading with him not to give her away.

"Officer Potter?" the librarian called.

"Hmm?" Potter looked up from his phone.

Annalisa held her breath.

"I thought I saw some kids heading out toward the football equipment shed," Torvald said. "I'm sure they're up to no good. You might want to go check it out."

"Thanks," Potter said, and headed up the hall in the direction of the athletic fields.

Torvald winked at Annalisa, who mouthed *thank you* back at him. She turned and flew up the hall. Her cape flapped behind her and she smiled. That was how it was *supposed* to be. She was flagrantly violating school rules, and she didn't care. She hit the doors at speed and nearly knocked them off their hinges as she flew out and angled herself toward the sun. She tossed her backpack onto the school's roof where she could retrieve it later and rocketed into the sky.

Aighleigh had found the schedule for the funeral, and sent it to Annalisa's phone. It would begin with a mile-long procession from the park where Dominic Ortega had been shot to the church where his memorial service would be held. Then the family would go with his body to a private burial while the rest of the attendees planned to march two miles to City Hall where they would call out the Mayor to address the issue of race-based police violence and to ask charges be filed against the officers who'd slain Ortega.

Annalisa saw the gathering of people. There were so many! When Malley Middle School had fire drills and the parking lot filled with students, it seemed like that many people were hanging around in the park. Some chanted while others sang something that might have been a hymn. She saw police off to one side, but they weren't wearing riot gear and seemed to be keeping their distance. Someone spotted her and pointed and shortly a hundred phones were raised to take her picture or shoot video. The attention made her want to turn around and fly away, but she'd committed to being a part of this, and she would see it through.

"I wish you were here, Breezy," she whispered. He lent her strength with his easy smile. She made herself smile and wave at the onlookers, then she raised her own phone to take a picture of the crowd from overhead. Vinnie would like that; it meant she was thinking big picture.

She studied the crowd for a minute until she found the group that appeared to be Ortega's family. They were all in black and surrounding a pickup truck that had been exquisitely detailed. It had broad wheels and low profile tires, shiny chrome detailing, and exhaust pipes that rose behind the cab like it was a semi.

A coffin rested in the back, surrounded by flowers with a picture of Dominic Ortega on an easel leaning against the truck's back window.

Annalisa dropped gently and respectfully to the ground beside the Ortega family instead of landing with her customary earth-shaking thump. She recognized Dominic's widow, Mrs. Ortega, from the picture Aighleigh had sent her. The woman was younger than Annalisa's mother, with luxuriant black hair gathered in a silver clasp beneath a veil. Her eyes were shadowed and Annalisa had never seen anyone who looked as sad. It made her own eyes fill with tears. "Mrs. Ortega? I'm Annalisa. I-I'm sorry about your husband. May I walk with you today?"

"Why you here, hero?" asked a heavyset Hispanic man with tattoos on the backs of his hands. The question wasn't a challenge, but Annalisa knew he had every right to ask. She was an interloper.

"I . . . I feel bad about what happened to Mr. Ortega. I got there too late to help him. I was at the . . . the protest last night. My friends got hurt. I know other people did too. I don't want that to happen today."

"You gonna protect us if the cops start hasslin' us?"

Annalisa sighed. She knew it would eventually come down to picking sides. "Yes. As long as you are respectful, I've got your backs."

"Jaime," Mrs. Ortega said in a voice hoarse from hours of mourning. "She's just a kid. She wants to help. Let her."

Jaime nodded and bowed his head. "Of course. Welcome, sister." He climbed onto the running board of the truck and looked out across the gathered attendees. He put his fingers to his lips and let out a piercing whistle that made Annalisa's ears ring. People looked in his direction and he raised one hand, circling a finger in a *let's go* motion. He slipped behind the wheel and set the truck rolling, keeping his foot on the brake so it didn't go any faster than walking speed.

Annalisa didn't know what else to do so she walked alongside Mrs. Ortega. The woman was quiet for a long time during the march. At last, after what felt like an eternity of listening to the thrum of the truck's exhaust pipes, Mrs. Ortega spoke. "How old are you, Capitána?"

"Fourteen, ma'am. I'll be fifteen in October."

Mrs. Ortega chuckled but wiped her eyes. "Please, call me Cherise. Dominic and I wanted to have children, but God must have not seen it that way. We tried for so long. We talked about adopting, but neither of us really knew where to begin."

"I'm . . . I'm sorry." Annalisa felt like her words were hollow, but Cherise took her hand.

"Don't apologize. You're doing just fine, standing up for us. For Dominic. It means a lot to have someone with powers on our side."

"I don't know if I'm on any side," Annalisa said. "I'm just trying to do what's right."

"Then you're on the right side." Cherise sighed. "I wish Dominic could have met you. I think he would like you very much."

"Tell me about him. What was he like?"

"He sang rhythm and blues songs in the mornings after he got home from work at the plant, before I had to go in to the store. Sometimes he'd sing them in Spanish. He loved Caribbean food. Nothing was ever spicy enough for him. Sometimes he'd eat so much of it that his stomach hurt all the next day, and I'd yell at him, but he'd just smile and rub his stomach and say pain went away but the memory of delicious food lasted forever."

"He sounds really nice."

"He was so kind. Dogs loved him. Even our neighbor's Rottie, who barks at squirrels and birds and growls at schoolkids, would curl up in his lap." Tears streamed down Cherise's face, and Annalisa was crying too. It hurt to hear what kind of man the world had lost. It hurt that she would never get to meet him. Cherise wiped her eyes. "Don't get me wrong. He wasn't perfect. He spent too much money on stereo equipment. He always had to have the newest, best system. We would fight about it. But then he would sing to me." A shuddering sigh escaped her. "I'll miss his voice the most."

The truck braked to a halt and Annalisa realized they'd arrived at the church. She wiped her eyes and looked back at the mourners behind them. They'd gathered a large crowd, enough that she wondered if the church would hold them all. Then she smiled a little through her tears. It didn't matter if the church was big enough; it would stretch to accommodate those who wished to remember Dominic Ortega, whether they had known him as close friends and family, as acquaintances, or even—like Annalisa—as people who only wished they had.

A dragonfly buzzed past Annalisa, humming in her field of vision just long enough for her to know she wasn't alone. Aighleigh was watching her. She reached out and took Cherise's hand. "Are you ready?"

"Oh, *amiga*, I don't think I'll ever be ready," Cherise said. "How do you say goodbye to someone you love?"

"I don't know. I've never had to." Annalisa shivered. She knew dying of old age was a privilege rarely afforded to parahuman heroes. She'd read so much about the heroes of Just Cause who had died in defense of civilians, or their friends, or even the entire world. They might not be household names for most of the world, but to Annalisa, they weren't just names, they were people. Mastiff. Johnny Go. Carousel. Orb. Stratocaster. Glimmer.

She tried not to think about her name, or the names of her friends being added to that list, but the chances were good that they, too, would eventually die with their boots on instead of peacefully. Being confronted by one's own mortality was a terrifying way to spiral into the black pit of despair.

She squeezed Cherise's hand, remembering to be gentle but trying to lend strength and draw it at the same time. "We'll be okay," she said.

They had to be.

Chapter Fifteen

The memorial service wasn't as grim as Annalisa feared. The preacher was a pleasant young woman with a powerful voice that carried clearly to the back of the church, even packed full of people with standing room only. She spoke about Dominic Ortega the man, not the symbol he'd become. She knew him personally, and told a couple anecdotes about him with such grace and humor that people chuckled despite the somber occasion. Annalisa found herself smiling and nodding along with the preacher.

They all sang a song together that Annalisa didn't know but she stumbled her way through it. Cherise told her it had been one of Dominic's favorites, about *how sweet it is to be loved by you.* There was prayer, and a period where people who wanted to say something about Dominic could do so into a microphone. Annalisa wondered if she should say a few words, but she hadn't known him and she would have felt like an impostor so she stayed seated beside Cherise until the very end of the service.

The preacher offered them all a blessing and bade them to go out and be at peace, even in the face of life's most difficult days. Even though it had been a service to commemorate a man who'd died from violence, Annalisa felt the stress of the past several days melt away. No wonder so many people had come, she thought. The preacher's words were as soothing as aloe cream on a sunburn.

"Thank you for coming, and thank you for staying," Cherise told her as people filed out of the church. "You didn't have to, and I'm grateful you did."

"I wanted to stay," Annalisa said. "I'm glad I got to meet you, Cherise. I wish I'd gotten to meet Dominic too."

"Someday you will, I'm sure," Cherise said. "I can feel him here. He's watching over me like my guardian angel. I'm sure he likes you too." She took a deep breath. "Would you like to come with me to the b . . . the next part?" Her lip quivered and Annalisa knew she was barely keeping herself together.

She almost said yes, but she had a greater responsibility and she knew it. "I would love to, but I can't. A lot of these people are going on to march to City Hall, and I need to go along."

Cherise nodded. "Of course. You have to protect them. It's why you are here."

"I'm . . . I'm sorry I couldn't protect Dominic." Annalisa hung her head.

"You can't be everywhere at once, Capitána. Nobody is blaming you. I'm not either. I'm glad you came along today. You made it a little easier for me."

Annalisa smiled and gave Cherise her number. "Take care, Cherise. You call me if you ever need me. Even if it's just to, you know, reach something on the top shelf." She raised herself a few inches off the ground. "I can reach it for you."

Cherise laughed. "I will. Go on, young lady. Be the hero these people need." She turned and left the church with Jaime.

Annalisa found herself alone in the church, which suddenly felt far less comforting than it had when the preacher had been speaking. She looked at the simple wooden cross on the wall above the pulpit and found no solace in its right angles. Cherise was right; she had people who needed her protection, and that was something she could believe in more than a god who let men like Dominic Ortega get shot in the back so they couldn't sing Marvin Gaye songs to their wives any longer.

Most of the funeral attendees also participated in the march to City Hall. They unfurled signs and attached them to sticks. The messages ranged from *JUSTICE FOR DOMINIC*, which Annalisa thought was perfectly rational, to the more extreme *STOP STATE-SANCTIONED RACIAL CLEANSING*. The marchers at the front of the group had bullhorns and they used them to lead chants and coordinate street-crossings. The leaders warned the marchers that if they blocked traffic, they would be subject to tickets or arrests. Police shadowed the group like wolves prowling through the underbrush, waiting for someone to make a mistake. The leaders were a pair of fiery young women, several years older than Annalisa but with the kind of crowd-management skills that would have made any school administrator jealous. They kept up a steady stream of instructions and warnings.

Annalisa flew over the marchers, staying low and drifting from the front of the pack to the rear and back again. Aighleigh's dragonfly conserved its power by riding on her shoulder. She could feel its tiny claws through her costume as they clenched on the fabric.

A lot of people were paying attention to the march. Cars passing by often honked their horns. The marchers collectively decided this was supporting their cause, and they cheered every time a horn blared. Occasionally someone would yell an obscenity out the window, and the marchers' cheers became angry jeers and retorts. Nobody started anything worse than that, for which Annalisa was profoundly grateful. She paid close attention to the emotional state of the group. If anybody seemed like they might be on the verge of getting out of line, she flew toward that person. She didn't confront the would-be instigator, because that wouldn't do anything except escalate the situation. She just made herself a visible presence overhead, a mute reminder of her power, and that seemed to have a mitigating effect upon the energy of the protest.

Annalisa saw several people were making their way through the crowd, armed with tablets and smartphones. They wore orange safety vests with the word PRESS spelled out either in Sharpie or with duct tape. Annalisa figured some of them were bloggers and others might be from local newspapers. There might even be some folks from big news outlets, but she wouldn't have recognized them anyway. She hadn't realized the funeral of Dominic Ortega would be such a big deal, but word seemed to have gotten out and people were taking an interest.

She checked her phone to see if Aighleigh had sent her any message, instead found one that made her heart flutter.

Breezys back yo.

Annalisa tried to convey all the complicated feelings she had to sort through in a single text. *Good*

2 see u here B. Her finger hovered over the SEND button, wondering if she should say something else; tell him how she really felt; how important he was to her. Instead she sent the message.

A moment later he replied with a simple smiley-face and it made her feel good for the first time in a couple days.

A *thupthupthup* sound of an approaching helicopter made her look up. A small 'copter from one of the Denver news stations was flying over the protesters, camera trained upon the crowd. That was good, Annalisa thought. It meant someone was actually paying attention to the events in a smallish town well away from the Metro Area. She locked eyes with the pilot and he raised his hand in a friendly wave. She waved back and he grinned. A young woman wearing a headset over her styled hair sat beside him, speaking toward a camera mounted on the side of the helicopter cabin.

The leaders of the march reached the steps of City Hall. A couple dozen police officers framed the edges, keeping an eye on the proceedings. They weren't in riot gear, but Annalisa could sense their nerves singing. The protest leaders conferred for a minute and then one of them raised her bullhorn to address the gathering throng.

"We're here today to ask the Mayor for justice for Dominic Ortega," she said. People whistled and cheered. "Dominic Ortega was murdered, an unarmed man shot eight times in the back by Loveland police. *Eight times!*"

Angry shouts erupted from the crowd and transformed into a *Justice for Dominic* chant. The police looked nervously at each other, and

Annalisa couldn't blame them. They were easily outnumbered twenty or thirty to one. If the crowd mentality took command, it would become another riot and a lot of people were going to get hurt. Annalisa wanted to do something but she had no idea what would make a difference. She floated higher in the air, hoping that maybe people seeing her might calm the situation.

The chant died down as the leaders raised their fists in the air and called for quiet. The helicopter circled overhead as the pilot and reporter took in the full spectacle of the protest. Annalisa wondered if they might be waiting for something bad to happen. Protests in small towns barely warranted a blip on the news, but a riot would be the lead story.

"We call on the District Attorney to file charges against the officers who murdered Dominic Ortega," the protest leader said through her bullhorn, eliciting more cheers and whistles. "We will not stand mute when one of our brothers lies dead."

The *Justice for Dominic* chant started anew.

The protest leaders turned to face City Hall. "Come out, Mayor Babcock. We demand you respond to us, your constituents. Mayor, come out. Mayor, come out."

The chanting protesters dutifully switched from *Justice for Dominic* to *Mayor come out.*

A couple of police officers stepped away from their posts and started to approach the protest leaders. "Put down that bullhorn," one of them shouted. "Or we will confiscate it."

Annalisa flew over the heads of the protesters to land on the steps between the leaders and the approaching officers. Unlike her descent toward the funeral, which had been respectful, this time she slammed down onto the cement hard enough to crack a piece beneath one heel. They would *listen* to her, by God. The police startled at her sudden landing but she held up her hands. "Stay back," she said. "This is a peaceful protest."

"Step aside," warned one of the officers.

"Cut it out, Hennesey," said the other. "She's just a kid."

"Kid or not, she's a parahuman and there are laws about what she can and can't do."

Annalisa's face grew hot with the two of them talking about her like she wasn't even standing in front of them. "There are also laws about what these protesters can and can't do, and they're not breaking any of them." She didn't actually know if that was true or not, but it passed what her mom called the *smell test*. She made a mental note to study up on what was permissible in a public protest later so she would know the facts.

The protesters had in fact ceased their chanting as they witnessed Annalisa's confrontation with the police on the steps. The crowd seemed to be collectively holding its breath, wondering if things were about to take a turn for the worse. The helicopter hovered overhead and Annalisa could feel the camera trained upon her. She knew whatever she did next would be seen not only by all the police watching her, but the crowd and the reporter in the helicopter and everyone watching the news as well. She had to clench her fists and press them against her hips to keep her hands from shaking. The dragonfly on her shoulder flapped its wings and buzzed away as Aighleigh took to the sky where she could better see what was happening.

Annalisa took a slow deep breath and shouted, "Mayor, come out!"

The crowd cheered and immediately took up the chant once more. Annalisa grinned, feeling she'd made the correct call. She waved the officers back. "Go on," she called over the chant. "Go back to your posts. We're not breaking the law. Go get the Mayor. She needs to talk to us."

Officer Hennesey's eyes widened, but he wasn't looking at Annalisa; his gaze went past her, at something in the sky. He looked shocked and frightened, and Annalisa whirled around to see what had drawn his attention.

A figure flew in toward them, shadowy in gray and brown even in the bright midday sun. A cape or decorative wings flapped beneath her outstretched arms and her raven-colored hair flowed out from beneath a full-face mask with a tinted visor shaped like a bird's beak. "*Murderers!*" she screamed. "*How does it feel to be afraid?*"

She had a weapon of some kind on her left wrist. She pointed it at the police and fired.

Chapter Sixteen

Annalisa didn't even have time to think as she threw herself into the sky to interpose herself between whatever it was the woman was firing and the police. She knew she was bulletproof, but if the woman had some kind of high-tech superweapon, it might be Annalisa's last mistake.

A stream of small metal spheres like over-sized BB pellets bounced off Annalisa as if they were no more dangerous than ping-pong balls. Maybe they wouldn't have killed the police officers; maybe they were only intended to hurt, but they didn't hurt Annalisa. The mystery woman had screamed *murderers* at the police, and Annalisa realized she had probably been the one who defaced the police department.

Beneath her visor, the woman's eyes widened in surprise as she found herself confronting the unexpected superhero. She wheeled about and flew off at a sharp angle, away from the police, twisting in mid-flight to make herself a hard target to hit.

Annalisa glanced down at the police and protesters. Many people had thrown themselves to the ground at the sudden, unexpected attack, and were only just starting to pick themselves back up and look around in shock. Nobody looked like they were hurt, and Annalisa was the only one who could catch the mysterious new parahuman. "I'll handle this," she shouted at the police, and lit out in pursuit.

Right away, Annalisa knew she had a real race on her hands. The other flier was faster than her, but she kept her altitude low. Annalisa knew her opponent was trying to lose her amid the trees and buildings. What Annalisa didn't have in speed, she made up for in area knowledge and a quicker turning radius. She managed to put those skills to work and kept up with the other flier.

The other woman's costume had a definite homemade look to it, reminding Annalisa of the costumes she and her teammates had worn when they first started out as the Neighborhood Watch. Even so, the costume appeared well-designed and had padding sewn into it for protection. Subtle swatches of fabric gave the outfit a textured look like feathers, a look further enhanced by the fabric wings running from wrist to armpit and down to the woman's waist. Unlike Breezy's voluminous cape, the woman's wings didn't appear functional, for she didn't need to flap or angle them when she dove or turned.

"All right," Annalisa growled. "So you can fly. I can fly too."

The news helicopter followed the racing fliers; Annalisa could hear it above and behind. She wondered how fast it could go. For that matter, she wondered how fast her opponent could fly. Annalisa only had a rough estimate of her own top speed, thanks to Aighleigh running speed tests and doing all the math for her. Ninety-two miles per hour was fast, but the woman ahead of her seemed like she was topping out at over a hundred.

The woman zipped up a street and cut through the park where Dominic Ortega had met his unfortunate end. Annalisa strained to keep up—or at least to keep the woman in her line of sight. She angled her flight upward through a gap in the trees. At least she'd be able to see the woman better from a higher vantage point.

Annalisa's quarry slowed and looked behind her, checking for pursuit. Behind Annalisa, the news helicopter approached at speed. The noise of its rotors drew the woman's attention and she spotted Annalisa. Behind her visor, she snarled and spun away, staying close to the ground where trees and buildings would make it harder for Annalisa to see her.

Annalisa yanked her phone from its pouch. It occurred to her that she should probably ask her parents for a Bluetooth earpiece so she wouldn't have to risk dropping the phone from a hundred feet up in the air. "Call Aighleigh," she said, hoping the phone's mic would pick up her voice over the rushing air. She didn't want to take her attention away from the fleeing woman even for the moment it would take to speed-dial her friend.

"Call Aighleigh, okay," said the phone, and dialed.

Aighleigh answered right away, sounding breathless and excited. "Is it a supervillain?" she asked.

"Yes, it's a supervillain. Tell me you're tracking her."

"I'm trying. I'm on the library computer. Torvald let me come in so I could help you. I'm going to be in so much trouble for ditching Science. On the other hand, I've got a hundred and thirty percent thanks to all my extra credit—"

"*Aighleigh, that's not helping!*" Annalisa yelled.

"Sorry! Okay, I just connected remotely to my home system. I've got her. She's heading east toward the Interstate."

"She's faster than me. I'm going to lose her. What do I do?"

"Fly faster!"

"Not helping!"

"Sorry again. It's not like she's in a car and I can change a traffic light to block her. Hey, you should—" The approaching helicopter drowned out the rest of Aighleigh's suggestion.

"What? I can't hear you because of the helicopter." And then, like a shot, Annalisa figured it out. The helicopter was faster than her because it had gained on her. It could catch the fleeing supervillain. She turned and waved at the pilot, then pointed in the direction of the fugitive and made a *hurry up* motion.

The pilot waved back and tilted the helicopter forward a bit more to increase its speed. Annalisa ducked beneath it as it passed her by and grabbed hold of one of the landing skids. The noise was tremendous and she wished she had earplugs. She clenched her teeth against the pain and held on as the helicopter dragged her forward, faster than she'd ever gone.

The camera turret spun to focus on her and she could imagine the reporter shouting about how they'd joined the pursuit. Annalisa's cape whipped behind her, tugging hard enough to make her keep her fingers tight around the landing skid. It was working, and they were gaining quickly on the woman in brown and gray.

The supervillain glanced back and her eyes widened as she saw the helicopter racing toward her. She slowed in her headlong flight, turned, and charged at the 'copter in a sudden attack.

Either the pilot was a fool or didn't realize how much danger he was facing. Annalisa gasped as the supervillain raised her weapon. She pounded on the helicopter's body, trying to signal the pilot to change course, but it was too late.

A stream of ball bearings hissed through the sky against the helicopter, sounding like hail on a car roof. Something cracked up by the rotors and the engine changed its pitch to a strained, uneven cough. The helicopter tipped to one side and the tail swung around. The motion made Annalisa lose her grip and she tumbled through the air for a moment until she got her flight under control.

The helicopter was falling!

It wasn't dropping like a stone. Instead, it was heeled over at an awkward angle as black smoke poured from the engine and the tail rotated around the body like a moon orbiting a planet.

All thoughts of the supervillain forgotten, Annalisa raced toward the helicopter. She had to save the pilot and reporter, and she had to stop it from crashing and maybe killing someone when it hit the ground. She didn't know how heavy helicopters were, or if she could do anything to save it, but she had to try. As she moved in toward the cabin, she saw the pilot's face contorted into a rictus of terror as he fought with the controls. The reporter had her hands clenched in a death grip around her camera controls. There was no way Annalisa could get both of them out while the 'copter was still airborne; she wasn't fast enough to get them safely clear. She might have been able to save one, but that would mean leaving the other behind to die.

Instead, she grabbed hold of the landing skid and shoved against it, trying to stop the helicopter's tumbling spin. "Come . . . on . . ." she screamed as she strained against the ungainly vehicle's momentum. It was the heaviest thing she'd ever tried to move. She couldn't lift it, because there was nothing for her to brace against. She had nothing but the power of her own flight.

They were past the edge of town and there were more fields than there were neighborhoods, so at least they likely wouldn't come down on a building, but there was a highway *right there*, and the vision of the helicopter crashing into traffic made Annalisa fight even harder against gravity and momentum. The ground rushed toward them all too quickly. She pulled with all her might, and the 'copter's fall slowed.

And then everything went horribly wrong. Annalisa's pulling on the landing skid caused the helicopter to tilt past its ability to maintain lift, and suddenly it was rolling beneath her. She screamed wordlessly, feeling her muscles pushed to their limit as she tried to keep the upside-down 'copter aloft.

They came down in the field of a sod farm. The main rotor chopped a great swath of muddy vegetation into the air as the blades first sliced, then caught in the ground. The transfer of rotational momentum made the 'copter's body swing around faster than Annalisa could react, and it flung her loose. Something heavy and sharp smashed against her back and the next thing she knew she crashed hard into the soft earth.

Dazed from the sudden impact, she staggered to her feet, seeing double. The helicopter was on its side, its main rotors folded and twisted. The tail section was a dozen yards away and Annalisa had a sickening feeling that it was what had struck her. Helicopters were basically giant flying food processors, and she was surprised and relieved that the rotors hadn't chopped her to bits. She guessed she was a little more than just bulletproof.

Flames flared from the engine compartment and she smacked herself in the head, trying to knock her vision clear. She still had to save the pilot and reporter. She didn't know if she could really fly yet—she was still horribly dizzy, but she managed to half-fly, half-run to the cabin. Both the pilot and reporter were still strapped into their seats, heads lolling sideways with bloodied faces and eyes shut. "God, don't be dead. Please don't be dead," Annalisa said as she tore the door away.

She got the reporter free from her seat and set her on side of the helicopter while she turned back to retrieve the pilot. His straps wouldn't come loose, so she tore them like they were strips of paper and lifted him clear. Carrying two people was awkward enough when she wasn't dizzy and they could help by holding onto her. With two unconscious—or dead—adults, the best she could manage was to wrap her arms around their chests under their arms and lift. She raised them up and teetered on the edge of the 'copter body for a moment. Flames licked at her back, threatening to set her cape on fire. She made herself fly a couple dozen yards away before she couldn't manage to stay aloft any longer. She sank to the ground, set her two charges on the grass, and collapsed beside them.

With a *whump*, the flames reached the helicopter's fuel, and the craft exploded in a fireball. Annalisa somehow managed to get herself between it and the civilians, taking the brunt of the shockwave and shrapnel as pieces rained down around them both.

The pilot's eyes opened wide and, surprisingly, the first thing he asked was if Heather was all right. The reporter groaned and shifted her position, coughing.

Annalisa found the energy to smile. "She'll live. And so will you, Mister."

"My name's Marlon," he said. "You just saved our lives, Capitána. Thank you!"

Annalisa rolled onto her back and closed her eyes. "You're welcome, Marlon."

She heard approaching sirens over the sound of the remains of the news 'copter immolating itself and knew that at least for the moment, things would be all right.

Chapter Seventeen

Annalisa sat in the back of an ambulance, a blanket wrapped over her shoulders, her feet dangling above the ground like she was an actor in a television show. She felt shell-shocked. How close had she come to dying when the helicopter crashed into her? What if being bulletproof hadn't protected her from other types of injuries? She could be lying dead out there in the grass by the smoldering remains of the news 'copter, a sheet draped over her body as medical examiners tried to piece together what had happened.

The fear was paralyzing.

She hadn't had time to think about things like her own mortality when she was focused on trying to save the helicopter pilot. Getting him to safety had been the most important thing in her world at that moment. Now the moment had passed, she was awash in her own fears. *What if she had died?*

Heather the reporter had already been carted away with a broken arm. Marlon the pilot was sitting in a second ambulance, like her, wrapped in a blanket with a water bottle clutched in his hands. He saw her looking at him and smiled. He had a cut on his forehead and a paramedic was gluing it shut. Annalisa had a paramedic attending to her too, but she wasn't hurt. They hadn't found any sign of injuries—no broken bones, no cuts or contusions. Not even a bruise. She should have been torn in half, or had her back broken, or any number of things that *should* have been immediately fatal. Instead, the paramedics weren't even sure if she had so much as a concussion. Nevertheless, they were treating her like a TV accident victim, which meant a blanket and something to drink.

The fire crews had put out the remains of the helicopter and police had already cordoned off the area from the accumulating crowd of onlookers. Annalisa could only see a few of them from her vantage point, parked along the side of the road, phones pointed at the accident scene. Their videos would spread across Twitter and Instagram and YouTube and soon the whole world would know about La Capitána, the teenage hero who'd saved a news reporter pilot from certain death. Then they'd dig a little deeper, as people on the internet did, and they'd find out she hadn't caught the bad guy, and they would judge her.

How did superheroes like Mustang Sally cope? She wished she could go ask her idol. Ever since she'd first discovered her powers, Annalisa had been obsessed with Just Cause and the commander of the main team in New York. When Mustang Sally had retired and come to the Hero Academy, it was even more exciting for Annalisa to know her idol was only an hour away in Denver. She would be teaching Annalisa in the fall. Maybe she could talk to Sally then about her fears.

Then she realized she didn't really have to wait. Half of the Neighborhood Watch was out of commission from the previous night's protests, and the other half was stuck in school with no way to get anywhere quickly. There was a mysterious new parahuman attacking police and potentially inciting rioting. Surely Just Cause could get involved in that. They responded to emergencies.

This was an emergency for sure.

"Annalisa!"

She turned to see her mother running toward her from her parked car. She'd left the door hanging open and had a police officer trotting after her. Annalisa felt tears roll down her cheeks. She was going to make her mom so upset, but she didn't dare leave without at least reassuring her first.

She threw the blanket off her shoulders and set her water bottle down on the ambulance bumper.

"Hey—" began the paramedic, but Annalisa was already on her way across the field.

"It's okay, it's my mom," she called over her shoulder, and then her mom's arms were around her and she buried her face against her shoulder.

"Oh, *hija*, I was so afraid when I heard."

"I'm okay, Mamá. I'm not hurt." Annalisa sniffled at the same time as her mom and almost broke up laughing at it. "But I saved Heather and Marlon." She glanced in Marlon's direction. He saw her looking and touched his hand to his heart and nodded.

"They said you collided with a helicopter. What happened, *hija*?"

"There was a supervillain, Mamá. She shot the 'copter and I caught it before it crashed. Well, sort of. It was heavy and awkward and I couldn't stop it. I slowed it enough that nobody died. It blew up, though."

Her mom stepped back to hold her at arm's length. "You're not hurt? Not at all?"

Annalisa shook her head. "Not even sore. But I think I might need a new costume." She motioned to the tattered cape.

Her mom laughed. "We'll get you one. I'm just so glad you're all right."

A paramedic and a plainclothes police officer stepped over to them. "Mrs. Torres?" the officer asked.

"Yes, that's me."

"Can you show me some ID before I release Annalisa to you? I know she knows who you are, but I have to follow procedure since she's a minor."

Annalisa's mom dug through her purse, extricated her wallet, and displayed her driver's license to the officer. He glanced at it just long enough to confirm what Annalisa was sure he already knew.

"Thank you. Do you mind if I get her statement about what happened here? Again, she's a minor and I can't question her without your permission."

"Go ahead." Annalisa's mom put her arm around her shoulders and held her close.

The police officer asked Annalisa a few straightforward questions about what had happened from the moment the supervillain had arrived at the protest to the helicopter's explosion. He took notes and recorded her answers with his phone. None of his questions seemed leading or implied anything except that he was gathering information, which put Annalisa at ease. She was afraid her involvement in the protests would bias police against her, but this officer didn't appear concerned about that. He closed his notebook and tucked his phone away. "Well, I think we're done here for now. If I have any other questions for Annalisa, I'll contact you, Mrs. Torres." He handed her his card. Annalisa glanced at it. *Michael Hinckley, Crime Scene Investigator.*

"Thank you, Officer Hinckley," Annalisa's mom said.

"Annalisa did good work today. She kept a lot of people from getting hurt." Hinckley smiled at her. "I've been asked to convey thanks from the officers at City Hall. I believe the Mayor and Chief of Police will likely want to thank her personally."

"Oh," Annalisa said, suddenly feeling small without her teammates at her side.

"There's not a mark on Annalisa," the paramedic said. "We looked her over and couldn't find any indication of injury. She's not exhibiting signs of a concussion and I think she is just fine. However, I would recommend you get her checked out by her doctor just the same. There's a clinic in Denver set up for treatment of parahumans if needed."

Annalisa's mom nodded. "Thank you." She and Annalisa turned to head back toward her car. "Let's get you home and into a bath, young lady. You've had a busy day."

"Mamá . . . it's not done yet."

"What do you mean?"

"There's a supervillain still out there. She tried to hurt people today." Annalisa swallowed against the sudden lump in her throat. "And she got away."

"So what, you're going to go after her? *Hija,* that helicopter is still smoking. What will happen the next time you find her, if you even can?"

"I have to try. She's trying to make things worse with the protests. She went after the police. She called them murderers. I'm sure she's the one who spray-painted their headquarters."

"Baby, you're fourteen years old. It doesn't have to be you. Let the professionals handle it. Just Cause is in Denver. They can find her."

"Mamá, I can do it. *We* can do it. Me and the rest of the Neighborhood Watch."

"With half of them out injured? I don't think so."

"Then I will go get help myself."

"From who?"

"Just Cause. Mustang Sally knows me. She'll listen."

"I thought she was retired."

"She's a teacher at the Academy. That doesn't mean she's not still a superhero. Just Cause will listen to her, and she'll listen to me." Annalisa took a deep breath. "This whole thing with Mr. Ortega getting shot and the protests and the violence is bigger than just me. It's going to just keep building until someone else gets killed, and I've got to try to stop it before it gets to that point."

"Why you, *hija*?"

"Because I'm a superhero too. This is my hometown. I can't let it fall apart. Please trust me."

Annalisa's mom hugged her tight. "Oh, I trust you. I'm just worried. I'm your mother. It's my job."

"And right now, being a superhero is *my* job."

"I know, *hija*. I'm so proud of you for it." Her mom wiped her eyes. "Go on, then. Go bring Just Cause back here."

"I will, Mamá." Annalisa turned to leave.

"Annalisa . . ."

"Yeah?"

"Do you . . . I could drive you. I mean, I left work for this. They'll understand."

For a moment, Annalisa almost said yes, but then she thought about how it would look for her mom to take her to Just Cause. She knew deep down that she was still a kid. Everything that had happened in the past hour had to involve her mother because she was, after all, a minor. But she was also fourteen, and as much as Annalisa loved her parents, there was nothing cool about them being the taxi service and hovering nearby.

Not when she could fly.

She smiled. "No, I know where to go, and I can fly faster than even you drive on the highway, Leadfoot."

Annalisa's mom laughed. "Get out of here, *hija*, before I change my mind."

"I'll be back before you know it, Mamá." Annalisa leaped into the sky, her ragged cape flapping behind her as she rose. Camera phones tracked her progress, and she heard a smattering of applause and whistles over the wind rushing past her ears. In the near distance was the gray ribbon of the interstate, stretching north and south. She could follow that all the way to Denver then cut across town toward the open space where Just Cause and the Hero Academy were located. She faced her right shoulder toward the mountains, put her hands over her head in the classic superhero flying pose, and lit out toward Denver.

Chapter Eighteen

Annalisa knew, in theory, exactly where to find Just Cause Headquarters. She'd spent many hours poring over satellite images of the facility, trying to guess what buildings held what parts of the base. She'd nearly committed the entire Wikipedia article on it to memory.

In practice, she kept checking the GPS on her phone as she flew along the highway, passing cars beneath her like they were standing still. Once, she actually fumbled her phone right out of her fingers and only through some skilled flying and a whole barrel of luck did she manage to catch it in midair before it could shatter the windshield of some unsuspecting motorist. After that near miss, she decided maybe it was safer for everyone involved if she flew a lot higher and off to one side of the highway.

Every flying superhero had their own technique for streamlining themselves in flight when they needed to maximize velocity. What Annalisa had discovered worked best was to put her hands over her head with the backs touching, like she was diving into a pool. By shaping herself into a human wedge, she kept her speed up without getting tired.

And she could get tired if she flew too much. It was like using any other muscle—too much exertion and she'd become exhausted. Instead of muscle pain from overuse, her energy reserves flagged and flying became strenuous, as if she were trying to fly in a much stronger gravity well than the Earth's. Eventually she'd lose the ability to fly altogether and collapse to the ground, shaking and weakened. The only way to regain her flight, as far as she knew, was to get some food, some water, and some rest.

As the crow—or rather, the *Halcónita*—flew, it was less than an hour from Loveland to Just Cause Headquarters. That wasn't nearly enough time for her to get tired from the effort of remaining aloft. Just the same, she paid attention to her strength reserves. She'd already had a busy day between the funeral, the march, chasing the supervillain, and saving the helicopter pilot. She wouldn't have been surprised if she'd been too tired to make the journey south, but she seemed to be doing just fine. Maybe she'd found her second wind. Or maybe her first one wasn't blown out yet.

The Denver Metro Area didn't have a clearly-defined boundary. One minute she was flying over fields and the next over neighborhoods that had sprouted up like patches of weeds, sprawling around commercial districts anchored by big box stores and fast food islands. There was a lot of air traffic in the region as jets in the pattern approached or departed from Denver International Airport. Annalisa lowered her flight altitude until she was well below the height where she might accidentally run across any airliner.

She checked her phone and the GPS informed her she was only a few minutes from her destination. And then she saw it!

There were four buildings: the motor pool/hangar, the dormitory, the training center, and the Command Center. Further to the north was the compound of the Hero Academy, where she would be spending the next four years if everything worked out the way she hoped. The surrounding open space was covered with prairie grasses, green from spring rainstorms. Sparse stands of trees dotted the sward, and as she approached, she even saw a herd of deer wandering the grassland.

"Hi there!" someone called, and Annalisa jumped midflight, which was a sort of airborne stutter-twist that wouldn't have looked like anything to a non-flyer.

She turned to see a young woman—or maybe just an older student—wearing short shorts, a tank top, and flying on a set of gorgeous dragonfly wings. She had short blonde hair with a couple of longer locks dyed green and purple. A pair of goggles rode around her throat. She smiled at Annalisa, who gasped as she realized who the newcomer was. "Oh my gosh, you're WyldWing!" WyldWing was one of the graduating seniors from the Hero Academy. When she'd been a freshman, the same age as Annalisa, she and her classmates had stopped an honest-to-goodness supervillain and saved a lot of lives in the process. Annalisa had read everything she could find about the event.

"Guilty as charged," WyldWing said. "I'm Chloe. Are you okay? You look like you've had a rough day."

Annalisa felt her cheeks grow hot as she really noticed her appearance for the first time. She was dusty from her flight. Her costume was scorched and smudged and had a bunch of rips and tears in it. "I, uh . . . there was a helicopter. I'm not hurt or anything. I'm, uh . . ."

"Hey, it's okay. We saw you approaching and I figured I'd come check you out before Just Cause called out the cavalry. They get suspicious about people flying toward the base when they're not expecting anyone. Do you need help?" Chloe flew closer to her. It wasn't a threatening approach; the young woman looked concerned.

"I . . . yeah, I guess maybe I do." Annalisa was feeling more than a little starstruck at meeting WyldWing in such an informal setting, and her body was giving her indications that she was too tired to remain aloft much longer.

"Come on down with me. We're having a bit of a party. It's graduation next week and we're done with classes and celebrating. There's hot dogs and chicken and grilled veggies if you're vegetarian. Soda. Water. Chips." She pointed at a gathering of people down by a lake. Her wings buzzed and blew air around Annalisa. She hadn't heard Chloe approach before.

"How come your wings are noisy now?" Annalisa asked. "You were quiet before."

"I learned how to sequence my wingbeats last year to minimize the sound. Sometimes sounding like a giant insect is more obnoxious than useful. I can't fly very fast when I do it, but it's good when I don't want to broadcast to everyone in the area that *WyldWing is on the way.*"

The girls flew down to the party where maybe a dozen people had congregated around a couple portable grills and folding picnic tables. Annalisa had never been so close to so many parahumans before, even when the Neighborhood Watch and the Culture Club had worked together once. And it was different now, because these were *real* heroes. They were about to head off to various Just Cause branches around the country to fulfill their destinies. One day, it would be Annalisa about to take that journey, and she couldn't wait.

"Who's your friend, Chloe?" asked a dark-haired girl toasting a skewer full of marshmallows with a ball of flame held in one hand without burning it.

"Everyone, this is . . . Oh my gosh, I never asked your name! I'm so embarrassed!" Chloe's wings folded down her back like an iridescent cape. She clasped her hands together and looked at Annalisa.

"It's, uh, it's okay. I'm Annalisa, but people call me La Capitána." Annalisa winced as she said it; it had never sounded so stupid before.

A handsome black boy with a goatee and a lightning bolt shaved into his hair snapped his fingers. "I know who you are," he said in a surprisingly gentle voice with a definite country twang. "You're one of those kids from up north. Neighborhood Watch, am I right?"

Annalisa nodded. Her stomach growled loud enough for Chloe to gasp, "Someone's been using her powers too long. Quick, Linds, get Annalisa a plate before she faints."

Annalisa protested, "I'm not going to—" Although, she had to admit, she did feel a little weak.

Chloe accepted a paper plate from the girl who'd been toasting marshmallows. It held a couple of hot dogs, some chips, and a pair of the freshly-toasted marshmallows. "You should eat those first before they solidify. Linds has a solid career ahead of her as a camp counselor if she washes out at Los Angeles."

Linds snorted. "My mom is already trying to get me to come back to the Six. I keep telling her, look, maybe I wanted to be a prison guard when I was five. But . . . God, it's *Montana*."

The black boy smiled. "Annalisa, it's nice to meet you. I'm Jacob, a.k.a. Calamity."

"Calamity Jake," said a short Asian American girl with muscles like a bodybuilder. "He's great at running but his stopping needs work." The others laughed but not in a mean way. "I'm Ava. Call me Flint."

"Like the rock?" Annalisa figured Ava was probably a brick like her. She carried herself with the confidence of someone who didn't easily get hurt and could move mountains when called upon to do so.

"Like my hometown. Detroit's got Detroit Steel, so Flint, Michigan's got me." Her smile faded. "It's important people remember that name. I know a lot of people who got sick from the water. And people who are still sick."

Annalisa was too embarrassed to admit she didn't know what Ava was talking about, so she took a huge bite of hot dog to cover it up.

"Lindsay," said Linds. "Fireball. I'm going to be on Just Cause Los Angeles."

"First we've heard of it," said Jacob.

"At least in the past ten minutes," added a girl with multi-colored hair. "I'm Rhiannon. Cacophony," she added. "I'm . . . loud. Hey, DaVinci, put your pencil down for once in your life and come be social," she called to a boy perched on a seat with his nose buried in a sketchbook. He didn't react so she raised her voice until she'd achieved a concert volume. "L.J., get your skinny ass over here."

L.J. set aside his drawing pad and came over to meet Annalisa. "Hi. I'm L.J."

"L.J.?" Annalisa asked, not sure she'd heard it right.

Rhiannon rolled her eyes. "Yeah, we've all spent four years trying to guess what it stands for. Nothing."

"Lunchtime Jukebox," he said. "I've been saving that one for a special occasion. Nice to meet you, Annalisa." He looked around. "Where's Maia? She's hard to miss."

Rhiannon cocked her head toward the lake. "Where else? She was complaining about the heat."

A swimmer breached the surface of the lake. She reminded Annalisa of a whale, and then she was immediately sorry she'd made the connection in her mind, because even though it had been an innocent thought, it would have read as mean. The girl was large—not just tall, but sheathed in a layer of fat that seemed to push out her bluish skin enough to make it look like it was stretched tight. Annalisa had seen overweight people whose skin seemed doughy and flabby, but despite this young woman's bulk, there wasn't anything flabby about her.

Her skin was hairless and shed water like duck feathers as she emerged from the lake, and it was distinctly blue, like she had a full-body tattoo or a really weird tan. Her face was broad and friendly, and she wore a black and white one-piece swimming suit that once again made Annalisa think of a whale, but this time because of the design. "Hello," the swimmer said in a husky voice. "I'm Maia, or Devilfish."

"What's a devilfish?"

"It's another name for a gray whale."

"Is that like a killer whale?" Annalisa asked.

Maia smiled. "Not unless you're a seal."

The scandalized look Annalisa's face must have been so epic that Maia, L.J., and Rhiannon all burst out laughing. Annalisa wished she had long hair so she could bow her head and hide behind it.

"You guys, stop picking on her." Chloe buzzed over to them. "She's just a kid. We were all there once."

"We're not picking on her," Maia said. "Who are you, by the way? I don't recognize you or the costume. And speaking of costumes, yours looks like it's seen better days."

"I'm, uh, Annalisa. La Capitána. And I had to stop a helicopter from crashing today."

"Did you?" Rhiannon asked, wide-eyed.

"Um, kind of."

"She's not kidding," L.J. said, holding up his phone. "It's all over the feeds. She saved the pilot's life after his 'copter got attacked by another parahuman. She's a hero, you guys."

Maia started applauding, and seemed completely sincere about it. The others joined in and Annalisa wished she could melt into the ground.

After what felt like an embarrassingly long time, the students' ovation ended and Chloe cleared her throat. "Well, now that you've got some food inside you, maybe you better tell us why you're here. I mean, you didn't fly all the way down here just to crash our party. Sorry, bad choice of words. You're totally welcome here."

"I'm . . . I guess I need Just Cause's help," Annalisa said.

"Well, you did better than that," Ava said. "You got us."

"We're practically Just Cause," Rhiannon chimed in. "Isn't that right, Los Angeles?"

Lindsay snorted. "You guys are hilarious."

"Pay no attention to these jackasses," Chloe said. "We've all got senioritis but that doesn't mean we're not here to help. What can we do for you, Annalisa?"

Chapter Nineteen

The Hero Academy had what Chloe called a library, but in Annalisa's eyes, it was seriously lacking in books. There were a couple shelves of books about parahuman powers, parahumans in history, and the like, but compared to Torvald's library, it was practically a desert.

She asked Chloe about it.

"We don't have a lot of time for reading for fun," Chloe said. "I mean, I'm sure some of the kids do, but a lot of us train in our spare time. I used to be a competing gymnast before I grew these things." She flapped her wings. "So I'm used to running all the time. I actually have a really hard time in regular school subjects, because I hate sitting down and focusing. I'd rather be flying, or training."

"I kind of like school," Annalisa said. "It's nice when you only have to worry about passing English and not about supervillains."

"Yeah, let's see what we can find out about yours."

Chloe had access to the Parahuman Resources Agency database, which was a clearinghouse of information on known parahumans. All Just Cause members had access to the database at any time, because one never knew when such information might mean the difference between life and death. Annalisa hadn't even known such a resource existed.

"We get access as seniors," Chloe said. "There's a lot of in-depth tactical training your last year here. They throw all these different theoretical situations at us and we have to try to come up with solutions. Sometimes they even set them up in the CSC for us to work through. It's pretty awesome. We're encouraged to examine the PRA database to learn about our peers around the country and throughout the world." She lowered her voice. "I kind of think it's partly in case we ever have to stop any of them." She smiled tightly at Annalisa. "Anyway, tell me about this supervillain. The system has a pretty robust search function. I bet we can find out who she is."

At Annalisa's direction, Chloe keyed in *FEMALE* and under known powers *FLIGHT* and when Annalisa described the weapon the woman had used, added *WEAPON* and narrowed it down to *TECHNOLOGICAL* and *PROJECTILE*. Then she frowned at the results. "Man, that's still a lot of names and pictures. Can you think of anything else?"

Annalisa screwed up her face as she thought. "Well, how many of them aren't American? I mean, mine doesn't have to be American, but it seems like a good filter."

Chloe clicked *UNITED STATES* and narrowed a list of several hundred down to several dozen instead. "That's more like it. What else? Got any costume details, if she wore one?"

"It was gray and brown. She had a helmet or a full-head mask, with a shaped plastic thing that looked like a beak. And she had, like, flaps under her arms. Like those flying squirrels."

Chloe selected colors on a spectrum, then marked *WINGS* and *CAPE*, *HELMET*, *MASK*, and *VISOR*.

Partial matches dropped away until only three remained. Chloe put up all three images so Annalisa could see them side by side. She recognized the one who'd attacked the police right away and pointed at the screen. "That's her."

Chloe opened the woman's file. "Annalisa, meet Cernícala. Kestrel, according to the translator. She ranks only a two on the Devereaux Index. Do you know what that is?"

Annalisa nodded. She'd read about it in one of the books Torvald had given her. It was a ranking of approximate parahuman power levels ranging from zero—normal humans—to nine, representing the most powerful parahumans. Annalisa had no idea where she ranked, but she was guessing probably only a two or three. She would have bet a four could have stopped the helicopter from crashing and a five probably would have caught the supervillain without any help. She tried not to let that get her down; she was still a kid.

"First appearance in 2016. Six public appearances since then, all in the Southern California area. Wonder what she's doing here? Oh . . ." Chloe pointed to a section on the report which had been filed by a member of Just Cause Los Angeles named Redwood, whom Annalisa didn't know. "Look at this. All her appearances have been at protests against police violence. She's got an axe to grind with the cops, looks like. They've got a possible civilian identity match based upon her first appearance."

Annalisa read over Chloe's shoulder. "Cristina Vargas. Sister of a victim killed in a police shooting. Disappeared before the funeral and Cernícala appeared shortly thereafter. She is a person of interest in the following cases . . ."

"Sounds like she might be following protesters around," Chloe said. "Which means either she's got a job that allows her to travel or she's unemployed and living on the kindness of other protesters. Someone might know where to find her."

"What's that?" Annalisa pointed to a name under the SEE ALSO heading.

"Blindspot." Chloe opened the link and it pulled up a picture of an unpleasant-looking white man with a shaved head and a tattoo like a crown of thorns around his scalp. "Hmmm. That's a weird ability. Selective invisibility."

"You mean like only some people can't see him?"

"White people can't," Chloe said. "That's a one on the Devereaux Index. Barely parahuman at all, really. There are Champions who rank higher. I wish they had a picture of him."

"They do." Annalisa pointed again. "It's right there. He looks like a jerk."

Chloe sighed. "I can't see him. He's like a vampire or something and can't be seen even in a picture."

"How does something like that even work, anyway? How does his power . . . know who to make him invisible to? How does it work on a computer?"

"I have no idea. It's probably psionic somehow. I know a guy I could ask about it, but I don't know if it would be very helpful. It says here he should be considered armed and dangerous. He is prone to inciting violence against minorities. Crap, he's been seen at three of the same events that Cernícala was."

"You think they're working together? Supervillains do that, right?"

"There aren't a lot of supervillains," Chloe said. "And I don't think they're working together. I think they're working against each other. They probably hate each other's guts. Cernícala joins protesters against police and acts out, and Blindspot retaliates against her and the protesters. Oh shit, Annalisa, he could be up in your town right now."

The idea was enough to give Annalisa the chills. She was afraid of white supremacists. Racism was bad enough when it was just harsh words and hate, but this guy Blindspot took more direct action. He was wanted in connection with eight assaults and two attempted homicides at various protests. He'd even been arrested once, and managed to walk out of a police station in Texas when he got the jump on the only two officers who were able to see him.

"I better go," Annalisa said. "What if you're right, Chloe?"

"Well, you're not going by yourself, that's for sure. I don't mean this in an unkind way, but you're still a kid. I'm practically in Just Cause now. Like, I'm literally only days away from shipping out to Seattle. Let me help you. Maybe Jacob too. We're the only ones who could get up to Loveland without needing a car. He'd be able to see Blindspot if he's around, and if the numbers on Cernícala's profile are accurate, I'm faster than she is. I bet between you and me, we could catch her."

"You'd do that? You and Jacob?"

Chloe grinned at her. "It's why we're here. Look, we know you've got protests going on up there, and people are getting hurt. Having a couple more eyes on the sky and boots on the ground will help calm things down."

"We are a little short-handed in the Neighborhood Watch," Annalisa said. "Breezy's recovering from, well, getting tased. And Rascal got a concussion."

Chloe waved at her. "Well, there you go. You need help. And it's the weekend now, so Jacob and I can leave campus unsupervised. Senior privilege. We'll jet on up to your hometown, help you with your supervillain problem, and be back home in time for our finals on Monday. What do you say?"

Annalisa thought about it, but not too long and not too deeply. "Okay, that sounds like a good plan to me."

"Cool." Chloe pulled out her phone. "Let me fill everyone in. They're going to be mad that they can't come along, but if we all leave, that's going to make the faculty suspicious."

"And that's against the rules?"

"No! Well, not exactly. Look, I'll take any heat that comes our way for it."

"That's not fair, Chloe. You shouldn't have to."

"It's fine, Annalisa. Me and Jake can help you out."

"Wouldn't it be better to have a lot of help, though?"

"Not if you want to catch Cernicala and maybe Blindspot too, if he turns up. The fact that the two of them have been free as long as they have means they're at least a little bit careful. They know when the law is getting close to catching up with them, and they fade away. This is a job for subtlety and speed."

Annalisa glanced at Chloe's wings. "Those don't look too subtle."

"They're not, but I can cover them with a poncho and nobody will know."

"I guess that works."

"Trust me." Chloe's phone buzzed and she checked the message, then chuckled. "Thought so. Lindsay's mad we're not bringing her, but she'll understand. Burners are about as subtle as an explosion."

Annalisa thought back to the time Cole had managed to ignite his entire body at once a couple years back. There hadn't been anything remotely subtle about it. "Yeah, okay. Hothead is like that too. So are we going?"

"Not quite yet. We need to grab some gear from Just Cause first."

"What kind of gear?"

"Sleeper sets. Lindsay showed me how to use them. Her mom is the warden at Deep Six." Deep Six was the underground prison for parahuman criminals. Annalisa had read all about it in one of Torvald's books: *Deep Six: A Decade Under the Ground.* "Also, we need to get you fixed up."

"What do you mean?"

"Annalisa, your costume is falling apart. There's a nanotech costume fabricator in Just Cause HQ. We'll get you looking sharp in no time."

"You guys don't sew your costumes?" Annalisa grimaced as soon as the words left her mouth. She sounded like *such* a rube.

"Not anymore. There used to be a whole costuming shop in the headquarters, but now they have a fabricator. It's the same tech they use in the Combat Simulation Chamber. Nanotech. It's the wave of the future. At least, that's what they tell me."

Annalisa looked down at herself. Yeah, she really was a mess. "Okay, I guess that's all right. How long does it take?"

"Is your costume made out of anything weird, or does it need any kind of special qualities?"

"I don't know what it's made out of. We ordered it online. I don't know what kind of special qualities it has."

Chloe smiled. "Then it won't take long at all."

Chapter Twenty

True to Chloe's word, the process of getting Annalisa a new costume was quick and painless. At first, Annalisa thought Chloe was going to take her into Just Cause Headquarters, which would have been the coolest thing ever, but instead the dragonfly-winged girl led her across the campus to the combat training building. "This is where the main team practices and trains," Chloe said as they entered through an upper-floor terrace. "There's no practice going on right now or we'd be shut out. That's a safety thing."

"They make costumes here?" Annalisa knew she sounded doubtful; she felt that way too.

"Well, kind of. They have fabricators that make training suits and armor and stuff like that. The main costume shop is in headquarters, but I think it would be better if they aren't involved."

"You're not supposed to be doing this, are you?"

Chloe touched down to the floor and folded her wings against her back. "Look, if this is bothering you, we'll scrounge something up from everyone's wardrobe. We all got Just Cause-spec costumes at the beginning of our senior year and we all have spares. We can outfit you. It won't look great, but at least you won't have to worry about your unitard shredding in midair."

"No, it's fine. I appreciate it." Annalisa shrugged. "Besides, I'm kind of supposed to be in school right now anyway."

"Here we are, just a couple of delinquents." Chloe cracked open the door from the antechamber where they'd entered and peeked through. "A fine couple of heroes we're turning out to be, huh? Come on, nobody's here."

The two girls went through the darkened building. "Won't they have security cameras and stuff?" Annalisa asked.

"Yes, but I've got that covered." Chloe pulled out her phone and sent a message on it.

"What's that?"

"My . . . friend Charlie is interning here in Denver. He's on monitor duty today, which is why he didn't come to our party. I let him know we're here." Her phone buzzed a message and Chloe smiled at what she read. "We're good."

"*Friend*, huh?" Annalisa hadn't missed the catch in Chloe's voice when she'd mentioned Charlie. She wondered if Chloe and Charlie were friends like she and Breezy were. Thinking of Breezy killed her cheerful mood. Her friend had been hurt and it still stung she hadn't been able to stop it.

"We were . . . younger. A lot happens in four years." Chloe cleared her throat.

"Are you dating anyone now?"

"It's . . . complicated. How about you?"

"Yeah. His name's Breezy. He flies, too."

"The black kid on your team? With the dreadlocks? He's cute!"

Annalisa laughed. "He'd be so embarrassed if he heard you say that."

"Well, I wish the two of you the best. It's tough getting involved with a teammate. Things can happen but the two of you still have to come to train every day together."

"You think we shouldn't be together?"

"I didn't say that. I said it's tough." Chloe led Annalisa through the halls and down a stairwell to a large, reinforced gymnasium. Overhead LED bulbs bathed the training room in bright white. Annalisa gasped in delight as she saw the floor moving like thick molasses. From all the reading she'd done and videos she'd watched, she knew it was a mass of nanotech machines, moving raw materials into place and constructing a training scenario like a giant 3-D printer.

"What are they making?" she asked, kneeling to get a closer look. She didn't touch the gently flowing mass; she didn't know if doing so might interfere in some way.

"I don't know," Chloe said. "They change training scenarios every three days to keep things fresh." She saw a couple technicians in the control room and waved. They waved back. "There. Now they think we're supposed to be here."

"I don't want you to get in trouble because of me."

"Don't worry, I get in trouble because of myself. Remind me to tell you about when I took off and flew most of the way across Kansas instead of being in school." They skirted around the edge of the Combat Simulation Chamber and into the auxiliary training rooms. There was a weight room, including some machines Chloe said were designed to offer resistance training for the super-strong. There was an armored shooting gallery to give anyone with a ranged attack or even a firearm marksmanship practice. Massage tables. Hot tubs and ice baths. Medical.

Finally, they entered the antechamber for the costuming scanner. Annalisa looked up at the large capsule-shaped booth with the low-tech privacy curtain. She had seen something very similar to it a couple years back when she'd spent some time with the Culture Club. Their fashion-icon mother had a body scanner that the triplets used to design their own costumes. "Do I . . . have to get naked?"

"You can leave your underwear on." Chloe went over to the control panel and studied it before touching a button. The capsule lit up and a hum filled the room. "I did when they did mine. Go ahead and get undressed and get in. Once you're scanned, the software will handle the costume creation. All you have to do is enter the parameters. Trust me, it's easier than it sounds. We're not all terrific graphic designers and costumers, but you should be able to recreate yours pretty handily. It doesn't look too terribly complicated."

"So I just wander around in my underwear while waiting?"

"Oh. Good point. Just a moment." Chloe sent a text. "I asked Jake to bring Lindsay's bathrobe. You're about her height and she won't mind. You can wear it while you wait. Don't worry, I'll make sure he doesn't look."

With a rapid-fire patter of footsteps, Jake rounded the corner, a white terrycloth bathrobe flapping at his side. He was barefoot, still wearing shorts and a tank top, and he skidded to a stop like a hockey skater, nearly losing his balance in the process.

"Easy there, Calamity Jake," Chloe said. "I didn't say it was an emergency."

"I'd have gotten here faster if it was." Jacob grinned. "Hi, Annalisa. Chloe gettin' you all handled?"

"Yeah. Thank you." Annalisa took the offered robe and closed the curtain.

"Out," Chloe said. "This is girls' time."

"I know, I know. I got a burger on the grill and it's almost time to flip it. Y'all comin' back to the party?"

"No, and you need to wrap it up yourself. You're coming with us."

"Oh?" Jacob sounded interested.

"Soon. Go eat."

"Two of my favorite words right there." He pattered away and was gone.

Annalisa finished undressing and stepped into the capsule. "What do I do?"

"Hold your arms up over your head, not touching it. Legs slightly apart. That gets the best scan. System says you're good. Close your eyes. Hold please."

Through her shut eyes, Annalisa saw bright green light play across her. She held her breath, afraid the slightest motion might cause the system to crash somehow.

"And we're done. Go ahead and hop out of there. Let's get your costume made."

"When the Culture Club made one for me, it took all night. How fast does this system do it?"

"For a basic costume, it's only a few minutes. Come over here and have a seat."

Annalisa wrapped the bathrobe around herself and sat where Chloe indicated. Chloe showed her how to scroll through costume options and colors.

"Obviously, there are a lot of customizations possible, but we're in kind of a hurry, so I wouldn't get too fancy."

"It's okay. My costume is kind of basic." Annalisa picked a green she liked and started with a full-body long-sleeved bodysuit in that color.

"Basic is good. Simple looks are powerful and memorable. That's why chest logos are still a thing even today."

Annalisa nodded. "I know. This is mine." She selected a white five-pointed star, gave it a heavy black outline, and tipped it on its side the way it was on her old costume. Red gloves, red boots, and a red cape.

"I love the cape," Chloe said. "Nobody wears those anymore. Classic. Oh, do you want pockets or pouches? Someplace to keep your phone, lip gloss, emergency feminine supplies? The system makes them streamlined so they're not bulky or ugly." She opened a previously invisible flap on her thigh and withdrew a slender phone. "Like it?"

"Oooh, yes, please!" Pockets had never sounded like such an amazing concept to Annalisa until she didn't ever have one when she needed it.

"Is that it?"

Annalisa nodded. "I think so."

Chloe hit the button marked PRINT and a timer at the top of the console began counting down from seven minutes. "Okay, so when this is done, you'll have a Just Cause-spec costume. It'll be made of armor fabric, resistant to fire and energy damage, and will stop a small-caliber bullet."

"I'm already bulletproof," Annalisa said.

Chloe stopped for a moment. "How do you know that?"

"I kind of got shot this one time. By a supervillain." Saying felt strangely nonchalant to Annalisa, like she was discussing a dress she'd bought or a movie she'd seen.

"You got *shot*? What are you guys dealing with up there in that little town? No, don't tell me. I'm sure I'm about to find out. Geez, talk about living a life less ordinary. Are you okay to hang out here for a few?"

"Where are you going?"

"I've already got a costume, but it's in my locker in the Academy. Jacob will probably want to wear his, too. It's got a helmet." She grinned. "Sometimes he needs it." She extended her wings and they blurred into motion, lifting her into the air. "I'll be back in a few."

"I'll be here." Annalisa sat on the chair at the control station and watched the progress of her costume being printed. She yawned. The events of the past week had finally caught up with her. She closed her eyes, just for a minute, she told herself sternly.

"Hey, Capitána, wake up, kiddo." Someone was gently shaking her and Annalisa sat up, wide-eyed in surprise as she found herself in unfamiliar surroundings.

Chloe stood beside her, garbed in a green and purple bodysuit that shimmered like insect scales. She had a pair of yellow-tinted goggles resting on her forehead, ready to be pulled down at a moment's notice.

Jacob stood beside her, wearing a black and fluorescent orange outfit with low-profile armor patches in strategic locations, over joints and internal organs. A helmet covered all but his lower jaw, with a visor to protect his face. Annalisa, who'd hit more than one bug while flying at speed, immediately understood the benefit.

"You okay?" Chloe asked. "We almost let you sleep, but you can't be comfortable in that position, and in all honesty, it would probably be better for you to go home and sleep in your own bed. Jake and I will come with you, make sure you get there safely. Then we'll look around your town for Cernícala and Blindspot."

"No," Annalisa said. "Not just you guys. I have a team. They'll want to help. And I want you to meet them." She stretched. "I didn't mean to fall asleep. It was just a catnap. What time is it?"

"Dinnertime," Jacob said. He held up a paper bag. "Can you eat while you fly? We packed you some leftovers from our party."

Annalisa's stomach rumbled loud enough for everyone to hear. She hadn't realized how hungry she was until Jacob mentioned food. She'd never actually flown while eating, but it seemed like an opportune moment to learn how. "I'm sure I'll figure it out."

Jacob smiled. "I envy you flyin' types. I can't eat while I run, and if I eat too soon beforehand, I get cramps. Basically, I'm hungry like all the time."

"My friend Breezy's that way. I've seen him eat an entire pizza by himself." Annalisa smiled at the memory. They'd had a pizza party for their birthdays, since all the Neighborhood Watch kids had birthdays within a couple of weeks of each other. Breezy had scarfed down an entire large pizza by himself and then laid on the couch in their converted-Winnebago headquarters groaning and moaning until even Rascal said teasing him wasn't any fun anymore.

"He gonna be around when we get there?"

"I hope so," Annalisa said. She pulled out her phone. She had a dozen missed messages from Aighleigh and one from Breezy. She skimmed all of them except for Breezy's simple *Yo*, disappointed it wasn't longer.

Everyone who can meet up in an hour, be at HQ, Annalisa texted into the Neighborhood Watch app. *Bringing help.* "Okay," she said. "Let's go."

Chapter Twenty-One

Annalisa had never before flown with people as fast as or faster than her. Breezy was the only other flyer in the Neighborhood Watch and although his winds could be pretty powerful, the faster they blew, the harder it was for him to control his flight as he was more or less subject to its capricious whims. The one time he'd tried to fly as fast as Annalisa he'd nearly splattered himself against the ground when his winds hit a pocket of heavier air and turned into a rapid downdraft. He'd spent a lot of time on the internet after that, learning about esoteric things like microbursts and wind shear and the like, and ultimately decided flying slower was safer in every way.

Chloe's wings blurred so fast they almost didn't seem to be moving at all, but she darted back and forth, dropping down to chat with Jacob and then floating back up to talk with Annalisa without any apparent effort. Annalisa asked how fast Chloe was and the winged girl said about ninety-five on a clear day with low humidity. Annalisa had never considered such things might matter but she supposed she would learn about it when she got to the Academy.

If Chloe was a speed demon, Jacob was even faster. He kept to frontage roads as much as possible, since barely-attentive drivers had a tendency to overreact when someone passed them on foot. Even in a state as cosmopolitan as Colorado had become, where the Hero Academy and Just Cause Denver meant superheroes were almost commonplace—if such a thing could be said —people still went a little nuts trying to take pictures. Nobody wanted to be the hero who caused an injury or death simply by using their powers to someone else's distraction.

They crossed the distance back to Loveland quickly. The hamburger and chips Jacob had packed helped her regain her strength, and the Coke—although it wasn't her preferred Mexican version—at least had given her a caffeine and sugar boost to keep her airborne.

As they flew, Chloe gave Annalisa her and Jacob's cell numbers, and Annalisa dropped a pin on her map app so the others could find the Neighborhood Watch headquarters. It was mostly for Jacob's benefit, as he was limited to the streets. His zig-zagging through town was every bit as quick as Chloe and Annalisa's flight over it, and they reached Aighleigh's dad's salvage yard at the same time.

"Oh, you guys have a real headquarters here!" Chloe said in wonderment as she took in the salvaged Winnebago and containers. "You're ahead of the game already."

Annalisa felt her ears get hot. "It's not like Just Cause or anything."

Chloe smiled. "It doesn't have to be. You're not Just Cause. You're the Neighborhood Watch, right? It's perfect for you guys. You'll always remember your time here." Her face grew sober and her voice wistful. "Being on a team is the best feeling."

"Oh, I don't know," Jacob said as he removed his helmet. "My grammy's deep-fried apple pie is so good you won't want anyone else around so you don't have to share."

The door to the Winnebago banged open and there was Breezy! Annalisa forgot she was supposed to be acting all cool and grownup in front of the *real* superheroes and squealed with delight. She flew across the yard in a flash to embrace him. "You're here! You came!"

"Hey, I wouldn't miss it," Breezy said.

Annalisa pushed him back. "You jerk, I was so worried about you. Aighleigh said you had to stay home today because of doctor's orders."

Breezy shrugged. "I'm feelin' okay. And I'm the one who should be callin' you a jerk. First you go off and fight a supervillain on your own. Then you blew up a helicopter. Then you up and went to Just Cause without any of us."

"I didn't blow up the helicopter. It just kind of . . . happened."

Chloe cleared her throat. "Annalisa, aren't you going to introduce us?"

Breezy stepped out of the Winnebago to hold open the door. "Y'all might as well come inside. AC's runnin' and my mom would say we're not payin' to cool the neighborhood."

Annalisa led Chloe and Jacob into the headquarters of the Neighborhood Watch, feeling like it was shabby and run-down after her visit to Just Cause. "Everyone, this is Chloe, also known as WyldWing. And this is Jacob. Um . . ."

"Calamity," he said with a smile. "I know, it's a little odd."

Annalisa introduced the other members of the team except for Vinnie, who wasn't there. "I guess he's still at home?" she asked Aighleigh.

"He is. He said he tried standing on his board and got so dizzy he fell down." Aighleigh's voice trembled for a moment. "He doesn't fall."

"He's the skateboarder, right?" Jacob asked. "I never got the hang of it. I always fell off. Being super-speedy and klutzy at the same time . . . well, there's a reason folks call me *Calamity*."

"Hey, did you get a new costume?" Breezy asked. "You look different. Like, in a good way."

Annalisa felt her ears pricking hot. "Yeah. You know, Laundry Day." She whirled and turned to Chloe. She wanted to be close to Breezy, but at the same time, she felt like it would be completely unprofessional, and besides, she didn't want everyone to see her being close with him. She began to understand what Chloe had meant when she said it was hard getting involved with one's teammate. "My other one got kind of, um, torn up," Annalisa mumbled.

Chloe jumped in right away and Annalisa could have hugged her for it. "So Annalisa came down to Just Cause to see if we could identify the parahuman who attacked the protest and helicopter. We helped her figure it out and came up to help."

"You're not in Just Cause," Aighleigh said. "You're still in the Academy."

Then it was Chloe's turn to mumble. "We're graduating. We've been assigned to teams."

Jacob twirled his helmet around in his hands. "We're here to help. And it sounds like y'all might need it. You're down a member, right?"

"Yeah. Rascal has a concussion. He got hit with a nightstick." Breezy crossed his arms. "And I got tased, but I'm good to go."

"You got *tased*, little brother?" Jacob's eyes widened. "Da-a-a-mn!"

"Why don't you start at the beginning so we know what's going on, and then we can figure out our next move," Chloe said.

Everyone looked at Aighleigh, who was their *de facto* leader when it came to all things related to data, but she shook her head. "No, this has to be Annalisa's story," she said. "Without her, we don't have the video, and we might have a couple friends hurt a lot worse than they were. And a dead helicopter pilot and reporter," she added.

"What video?" Chloe asked.

Everyone looked at Annalisa.

"Right after the police shot Dominic Ortega, I flew overhead. I got video of the officers talking about getting their stories straight," Annalisa said. "It's, uh, it's pretty disturbing."

Jacob frowned. "Sounds like it. This is the first I heard about it, though, and I've kind of been followin' the news about this. All I've heard is that the officers got suspended and there's an investigation and some protests. Do y'all know anything else about this?"

"That's all anyone knows," Aighleigh said. "Either on or off the record, nobody's talking about it."

"They should be talking about it," Chloe said. "It's not okay for police to kill unarmed civilians."

"But it still happens all the time," Jacob said. "This kind of hits close to home, know what I mean? There was, like, a meme a couple years ago. I was in it. Black Lives Matter people decided to make me their poster child when I saved some kids from a flood."

"I remember you now," Aighleigh said. "There was some . . . some racist stuff online about it too, wasn't there?"

Jacob looked at the floor. "Yeah. I . . . I don't much like to talk about it."

"Truth." Breezy sounded to Annalisa like he was trying to deepen his voice a little, to sound a bit older. She felt conflicted over it, because although it was good he was trying to be a little more mature about the situation, she kind of liked him better when he was just being his regular, goofy self. She resolved to talk to him about it when they had some time to sit down and chat.

Chloe squeezed Jacob's arm to comfort him. "So what about this video?"

"We haven't shown it to anyone," Aighleigh said.

"Why not?" Chloe asked. "If it's incriminating, and it shows police conspiring to cover something up, you're withholding crucial evidence. That could mean the difference between killers paying for their crimes or walking free." Jacob's mouth dropped open in astonishment. "What? I paid attention in Intro to Criminal Law."

"I mean, yeah, I did too, but you sound like an episode of *Law and Order*."

Chloe shrugged. "My mom's an attorney." She turned to Annalisa. "Can we see the video?"

Aighleigh queued it up on one of the big screens. "Bathroom's right behind you if you need to puke. It really is that kind of upsetting."

She pushed PLAY and Annalisa reached out for Breezy's hand. She needed the comfort of his fingers wrapped around hers.

Chloe and Jacob stayed silent as the video played. Her lips curled in disgust at the officers' words, while muscles twitched in Jacob's cheeks as he clenched his teeth in what seemed to be barely-restrained fury.

The video ended and Annalisa felt like she should apologize to her new friends. After all, she'd crashed *their* party and now they were in the middle of it all when it wasn't really their problem to solve. She was trying to figure out how to broach the subject when Chloe said, "You have to share this."

"Are you crazy? We've already had protests that nearly turned into riots," Aighleigh said. "If this gets out, you're going to have people setting cars on fire and targeting the police. That's already going on with Cernícala. We can't give her enough of a reason to attack the police again. What if she comes through with something more lethal than a BB gun?"

"Maybe show it to the Mayor? The Chief of Police? The District Attorney?" Chloe asked. "They need to know that whatever those two officers said in their report, this is something that actually happened."

"They ain't been charged with anythin'," Breezy said. "My mom is all kinds of mad about it."

"She should be," Jacob said. "They killed that man. They need to pay for that."

"Right on," said Breezy.

"It's after five on a Friday. Mayor's probably home," Cole said. "And we don't know where she lives or her personal phone number."

Aighleigh cleared her throat. "Well, actually . . ."

Chapter Twenty-Two

A lot of police were waiting outside City Hall when three-fifths of the Neighborhood Watch arrived, with Chloe and Jacob filling in for Vinnie, who was still at home nursing his concussion, and Cole, who didn't want to be carried around like a sack of potatoes and stayed behind to keep an eye on Aighleigh's cameras. If Cernícala showed her face somewhere around town again, he would alert the team.

Unlike earlier, when the police had been in their basic duty uniforms, now they were outfitted in full riot gear, with plastic shields and short, ugly rifles of some kind. It made Annalisa nervous—not because she was afraid she might get shot, but because she was afraid one of her less bulletproof friends might. Specifically she was worried about Breezy, and all she wanted to do was wrap her arms around him and protect him from harm.

The police had a couple of big spotlights set up on the steps of City Hall and had them sweeping across the sky even though the sun had barely dropped behind the mountains. Annalisa and Breezy wore their full costumes, colorful and hopefully recognizable to all the police protecting the streets. Below them, Jacob trotted along beside Aighleigh as she clomped along like a cyborg centaur.

Mayor Babcock had been super suspicious when Aighleigh had reached out to her, but she knew the Neighborhood Watch, and probably everyone in town knew how Annalisa had saved countless lives when she'd gone after Cernícala to protect the police. They were trading on that reputation to have the after-hours meeting they needed.

Before they'd left headquarters, Aighleigh had surprised them all with some neat little Bluetooth earbuds and mics that worked with their phones and connected them all through the Neighborhood Watch app. To transmit on the open frequency, all any of them had to do was touch the button on the outside of the earpiece.

"Sick," was Breezy's comment, which illustrated everyone's appreciation of the new tech.

Aighleigh had spares she gave to Chloe and Jacob. "I know Just Cause has gizmos like these, but we have our own setup." She had them each install the Neighborhood Watch app on their phone. "I guess that makes you honorary members."

"Sounds good to me," Chloe said. "We're honored for sure. You guys really have this superhero thing down."

"I hope we can live up to it," Jacob said, without sounding at all like he was mocking them.

"Heads up, we been made," Breezy said as several police officers spotted them on approach. A couple raised their weapons from resting positions but were warned to put them up as spotters identified the Neighborhood Watch.

"Keep cool, everyone," Aighleigh said. "The police are nervous. They got attacked only hours ago. Don't give anyone a reason to overreact."

"Yeah, we wouldn't want that," Breezy grumbled.

An officer in plainclothes and a vest waved at the flyers, motioning them to come over to him.

"Here we go," Annalisa said.

She, Breezy, and Chloe descended to the ground where Aighleigh and Jacob joined them. They nodded at each other and approached the plainclothes, who was flanked by a pair of large men in full SWAT gear.

Aighleigh stepped forward, her mechanical legs working as well as Annalisa had ever seen them. The plainclothes looked the group up and down. "You're the, uh, the Neighborhood Watch?" He looked like saying the words were physically painful.

"Most of us," Aighleigh said. "WyldWing and Calamity are here to help out. They're from Just Cause." It was a small white lie, but they were only a week from graduation and that was close enough. "We're here to meet with the Mayor."

"Well . . ." the plainclothes drew it out, the way adults did when they were about to deny something without coming right out and saying it.

"She's expecting us," Annalisa said.

"That's why we're here, and it's probably why you're here," Aighleigh said. "Can you please let Her Honor know we've arrived?"

Almost on cue, the plainclothes' radio crackled. "Two David Fourteen, come back."

The officer sighed and unclipped the handset from his shoulder. "Riley. Go ahead."

"The Mayor wants to see the capes. Send them in."

"Capes," Annalisa muttered. "That's cute."

"We do have capes," Breezy said. "Maybe it ain't personal."

Annalisa looked up at Riley and the two musclebound men flanking him. "Maybe," she said, but she didn't believe it for a moment.

"You kids can go on inside. Someone will meet you there and take you the rest of the way." Riley paused. "No funny business, understand?"

"Oh, we wouldn't dream of it," Aighleigh said, in a tone that suggested exactly what she thought of Riley's bluster and empty threats. "Now if you big, strong officers wouldn't mind stepping aside to let the crippled girl through . . ." She clopped her four feet daintily on the cement, as if dancing across hot coals.

Riley and his goons stood aside to let them pass. Breezy glared at them with naked hatred and Annalisa had to gently squeeze his hand to keep him from saying anything that might get them all in trouble.

The group crossed the street and headed up the steps. Annalisa wondered if she might have to help Aighleigh, but her friend's quadropede carried her up with no fuss or drama.

"That's a pretty cool way to get around," Chloe said. "And you made it yourself?"

"Yeah. It's kind of my thing," Aighleigh said, blushing to the roots of her hair.

"That's awesome you can do that. Gadgeteer powers are super rare. I think there have only been a half dozen people who had them since they started tracking powers," Chloe said.

"They call it *electromechanokinesis* or *technopathy* or *technomancy*," Jacob said in an offhanded way. Chloe gaped at him and he smiled. "What? You aren't the only one who studied!"

The group laughed as they reached the entrance to City Hall. More police officers stood guard by the double doors. They looked at the teens, expressions of doubt and distrust plain on their faces. "I don't suppose it's worth asking any of you for identification," one said.

"Actually, I have my ID." Chloe produced a card from a pocket of her suit. Jacob likewise displayed one.

The officer looked at them, and then back at Chloe and Jacob. "Are you the real deal?"

"Yes indeed," Chloe said. "These are our temporary cards. We'll get badges once we get to our assigned teams. I'm going to Seattle, and Jake is going to Dallas."

The officer shrugged and returned their ID cards. "Whatever, I guess. The Mayor's expecting you. Please follow me."

The five young heroes followed the officer into City Hall. Aighleigh took the lead as was typical for her. Annalisa stayed beside her, feeling like she was in over her head. Breezy was right behind them, carrying his oversize cape over his arms so it wouldn't drag on the floor. As good as it worked for him out in the open, it was a tripping hazard indoors. Maybe when they got to Just Cause finally, the costumiers could design a cape that stretched or shrank when not in use or something so it wouldn't be awkward for him. The two Hero Academy soon-to-be graduates brought up the rear. Annalisa kind of wished Chloe would walk beside her. She was enamored of the young winged woman—she admired Chloe's poise and confidence and hoped she might gain her own some day.

Mayor Babcock was waiting in a conference room with several other adults Annalisa didn't know and one she did—the Chief of Police. This was it, she thought. This was their Big Moment to show they were more than just a group of meddlesome kids. They were heroes, and what they did mattered.

"Wheels, La Capitána, Breezy, welcome," Mayor Babcock said. "And also, welcome to your two friends, I believe your names are WyldWing and Calamity?"

"Yes, Your Honor," Chloe said.

"I'm Barbara Babcock, Mayor of this city. It's a pleasure to meet you." She proceeded to introduce the others in the room. Annalisa didn't remember their names so much as their positions. The Deputy Mayor was a nondescript balding white man with close-cut gray hair in a fringe around the back of his hair. The District Attorney looked like he might have stepped out of a TV show, with an expensive suit and immaculately-styled hair. There were a couple aides and assistants, and of course, the Chief of Police. He wore a suit with a badge clipped to his belt and his mustache was by far his most memorable feature.

"Before we begin, I'd like to thank you, La Capitána, for your assistance earlier today. We can't count how many additional lives you saved through your actions, but I know there are a pilot and reporter who are thanking their lucky stars you were present to save theirs."

"Was, uh, was anybody else hurt when Cernícala attacked?"

"Cernícala." Babcock rolled the word around in her mouth like she was trying on a pair of shoes. "That's an odd name."

"It means Kestrel," Annalisa said.

"Why doesn't she call herself *Kestrel* then? No matter," the Mayor said. "I assume you've brought in help from Just Cause to track her down to keep her from causing any more problems?"

"Yes, that's part of it," Aighleigh said. "But there's more, Madam Mayor. The protests are getting more dangerous for everyone and we're hoping we can maybe help put a stop to them before anyone gets hurt worse. Cernicala isn't the only rogue parahuman who tends to show up at events like these. There's another one, a man called Blindspot, who is even worse."

The Police Chief cleared his throat. "I've heard of him. He's invisible, right?"

"Only to . . . well, to Caucasians," Aighleigh said.

"That means white folks can't see him," Breezy said. "Y'all need us to look out for him. And that means we can't be lookin' over our shoulders to make sure we ain't gettin' shot at . . . or tased."

"Now just a damn minute—" the Police Chief began.

"Hold on, Robert. He's right, however indelicately he may have put it," Babcock said. "Tell me more about what you know about Blindspot and . . . and the other one whose name I can't remember."

"Cernicala," Annalisa said. "She's drawn to protests, like what's going on here in town. We think she's probably the sister of a boy who was shot and killed by . . . um, by police." She glanced at the Chief of Police, whose expression was wholly disapproving.

"And Blindspot is a white supremacist who escalates protest situations by targeting protesters," Aighleigh said. "With his powers, and the lack of minorities in a lot of police departments, he's proven very hard to catch and to keep."

"And you have evidence that he's here in Loveland?" Babcock asked.

"No, but given his history, I would bet if he isn't already, he's on his way. Escalating protests and hurting minorities is his thing. He wants the chaos. He wants to see cops putting people in the hospital," Aighleigh said.

"Or worse," Breezy added. "All those so-called nonlethal weapons can kill black folks just as easily as not. Or they die in custody. We've all seen it happen."

"Breezy," Annalisa said softly. "You're escalating too."

"I'm just tellin' it like it is. Brothers die first, like Dominic Ortega." He nodded toward Jacob. "He knows. He's seen it too."

Annalisa glanced at Jacob, who was clearly struggling to keep his emotions in check. The Police Chief was clenching his fists and things were about to get out of hand if somebody didn't do something. "Mayor Babcock," she said quickly. "We need to show you something. We need to show all of you what happened when Dominic Ortega was shot."

"What do you mean, show us?" Babcock asked.

"There is no video of what happened," said the Police Chief. "The officers weren't wearing body cameras and everything happened outside of the range of their cruiser cams."

Annalisa shook her head. "There is a video, and I know because I took it myself."

The silence that followed her statement was so deafening it was like someone had hit MUTE on a remote control.

"What exactly do you mean, Capitána?" The Mayor asked into the silence.

"I mean I flew over to see what was going on after I heard the shots, and when I saw the two officers talking over . . . over Mr. Ortega's body, I took out my phone and recorded it."

Another long silence filled the air as aides and assistants glanced at each other. Mayor Babcock and the District Attorney both shot looks of deep suspicion, first toward Annalisa, but then they turned those gazes toward the Police Chief. "Capitána," the District Attorney said. "May we please see that video?"

"Now hold on just a goddamned minute," said the Chief. "She's just a kid. You can't just—"

"Robert, I am the Mayor of this city, and I can *just* anything I want if it will stop someone from holding a match to the powder keg." She turned to Annalisa. "Please, show us the video."

Annalisa pulled out her phone. "It's kind of a small screen. I'm sorry." She felt a hand on her arm and looked down to see Aighleigh smiling.

"It's okay, Annalisa. I got this." She motioned to the large television on the conference room wall. "Your Honor, would you please turn that on? I, uh, haven't got the remote control code worked out for it yet."

"You've been hacking while we've been talking?" Annalisa asked.

Aighleigh shrugged and smiled. "I multitask."

Mayor Babcock raised a remote and turned on the TV. It showed the first frame of the video Annalisa had shot, with Dominic Ortega lying lifeless on the ground below and the two officers who'd shot him staring at their handiwork. "Jesus Christ," she whispered.

"This is pretty upsetting," Annalisa said. "I've seen it more than anybody else here, and it doesn't get any easier."

Breezy took her hand. "I got you, babe." He squeezed her hand and she squeezed back.

Aighleigh played the video.

Chapter Twenty-Three

Annalisa waited while Mayor Babcock flushed the toilet and came out from the stall, shaky and pale. She staggered over to a sink to splash water on her face.

"It's okay, Mayor," Annalisa said. "It's really hard to see. I puked too."

"I—I didn't want to believe it. I wanted to believe our police were honest . . . honorable . . ." Babcock spat into the sink and splashed more water on her face.

Annalisa waited. She didn't know if she should say something or not, but she felt like she was on the cusp of an important decision, and she was terrified of screwing it up somehow.

The Mayor shut off the sink and looked up at herself in the mirror. Her eye makeup had run, making dark streaks down the wrinkles around her eyes. Her bun had come halfway undone and wisps of hair fluttered around her face like cloud streamers. "God, I'm a mess. My whole city's a mess. How did this happen?"

Annalisa stepped across the bathroom to stand beside her. "Mayor, it's not your fault. It's not everyone. It's just those two officers. They made a . . . a terrible mistake and a man paid for it with his life. It's not about what happened before now. It's what you do next that matters."

Babcock pulled her half-undone bun out, sending a half dozen bobby pins flying across the bathroom. "Well, shit." She gave up recreating the bun in favor of a simple ponytail. It made her look more approachable, Annalisa thought. "Capitána . . . Annalisa, isn't it?"

"Yes, Mayor."

"Please, call me Barb."

"Okay, uh, Barb."

"If you were me, Annalisa, what would you do now?"

Annalisa scrunched up her face. "I don't know. I don't know what Mayors are supposed to do at times like this. I know that people sometimes look up to me and my friends, because we have powers and—and costumes . . . but we're just trying to do the right thing. We aren't any better at making decisions than anyone else. I've made lots of bad decisions. I'll probably make a lot more bad ones."

"I've made a lot of bad decisions too, Annalisa. I don't know if the one I'm about to make will be for better or for worse, but I hope people look back on it as a good decision. Will you walk back to the conference room with me?"

"Um, yeah, of course."

The Mayor's shakiness seemed to have worn off as she strode from the bathroom, full of purpose. Her heels clacked on the hall floor. Heads poked from the conference room door, watching as the Mayor came back with Annalisa at her elbow. She entered the conference room and conversation died immediately as she took her place at the head of the table. The final frame of Annalisa's video remained on the screen behind the Mayor, still showing Dominic Ortega's bullet-riddled body.

Babcock looked around the room at those gathered, from the costumed heroes to the assistants to the Chief of Police.

"Ladies and gentlemen, what we've seen here today is terrible, and I will not stand on the sidelines any longer. Robert . . ." She turned her attention to the Police Chief, who looked utterly miserable. The corners of his mouth turned down beneath his walrus mustache and Annalisa was pretty sure he would have sunk right through the floor if he had the power to do so. "I want those two officers arrested and charged. Ben, can you get the paperwork handled for that?"

The District Attorney nodded. "You got it, Barb. I can have a warrant for you in ten minutes."

"You have something to say, Robert? You want to argue with me?" Mayor Babcock crossed her arms.

"No, Barb. I saw the same thing you did. You know I'll back up my men to hell and back, but I can't let this go. I can't say they didn't believe their lives were in danger when they opened fire, but that's a damning video. I'll send some uniforms to round up Phelps and Hembeck." The Police Chief stared at his clasped hands on the conference room table and wouldn't meet the Mayor's gaze.

Annalisa's heart hammered in excitement. They'd done it. They'd won! At least, she was pretty sure they had. She glanced in Breezy's direction and his white teeth flashed in a smile.

The Mayor looked toward one of her aides. "Jen, prepare a statement. As soon as those officers are in our custody, I want the word put out that we have arrested and charged them in the death of Dominic Ortega. They will be prosecuted. We've got to get that out to the protesters however we can. Maybe we can stop things from blowing up any worse." She turned to Aighleigh. "Wheels, I know Rascal has an exceptional social media footprint. Can I ask for his help in disseminating the press release?"

Aighleigh's eyes narrowed in suspicion but she nodded and said she would arrange for it, since he wasn't with them at the moment. Annalisa desperately wanted to ask Aighleigh what was bothering her, but short of dragging her friend back down the hall to an emergency meeting in the bathroom, didn't see any way to do so without arousing everyone else's suspicions.

"Now as far as this video goes, I need you to keep it under wraps. Do you understand? We're going to prosecute these officers for their actions. That video is evidence. If you leak it to the public, you're going to make it very difficult for those men to receive a fair trial."

"You're asking us to keep this a secret?" Aighleigh asked. "Doesn't the public have a right to see this?"

"Why have you kept it to yourself until now?" the District Attorney asked. "You've got that kid on your team with tens of thousands of followers. You could have made this go viral at any point."

"We didn't know if it was what we should do or not. I mean, we didn't know if we were going to make things worse by sharing it or not. Then we all got too busy to really talk about it," Annalisa admitted. "Right after I shot it the protests started, and then Breezy and Rascal got hurt, then was the funeral and Cernícala. I guess we didn't really have time to make a decision on it either way."

"There's a copy on my server," Aighleigh said. "And backed up in the cloud. You couldn't stop us if we decided to release it."

"What do you think would happen if you did?"

"Folks would see the truth about what happened," Breezy said. "They'd know those cops shot Ortega."

"They might riot," Chloe said. "I can tell emotions are running really high right now. Something like this would be like setting a match to a fuse."

"We don't want things to escalate any further," Babcock said. "I haven't called in any reinforcements from other departments and I don't want to, but if we wind up with full-scale rioting here, I'll have to. Then people *will* get hurt."

"If y'all wind up with riots, Just Cause will intervene. Civil defense is part of our charter," Jacob said.

"Escalation," repeated the Mayor. "I honestly don't like having parahumans involved at all. I believe it undermines the authority of the police department, but like it or not, I need them. At least when it comes to the Neighborhood Watch, they are well-known here. No offense, but beyond the really famous heroes, most people have no idea who's on which Just Cause team. I don't even think I know who's leading the Denver team, and that's in my own state."

"Snapdragon," Annalisa said. She shrugged when the Mayor looked at her. "What? Some people follow sports teams."

The District Attorney's phone rang and he stepped away from the table.

"The point is that if you release that video to the public, things will spiral out of control very quickly because as this young lady with the wings pointed out, emotions are running high. I can't let my town come apart at the seams because of a series of poor decisions. What I—what *we* really need is for you to find Cer . . . Cern . . ."

"Cernícala," Aighleigh said, not bothering to hide her sigh of exasperation.

"Yes, her, and to make sure that Blindspot fellow isn't going to stir things up worse. Ben, how are we looking?"

The District Attorney gave her a thumbs up as he disconnected his call. "Warrant's coming any moment from the judge." His phone dinged with an incoming message. "And we're on."

"Robert, I want those officers in custody as soon as possible. Keep it quiet. We don't want anything to happen until they are safe behind bars. We don't need a mob deciding to hand out its own justice," Babcock said.

"They ain't a mob," Breezy said. "They're just folks like you and me, Mayor. But they're mad, because another brother's been shot dead for no reason."

"We don't know that—" began the Police Chief.

"Quiet, Robert. Breezy has a point. I need you to broaden your perspective here. The best thing we can do is announce our intent to prosecute the officers for their actions. Yes, that doesn't guarantee a conviction, but at least it will show the people that we're not ignoring them. It shows them that the police aren't above the law," Babcock said.

"*Protect and serve,*" Annalisa said. "It seems like some officers aren't remembering that."

Breezy nodded at her.

"Robert, is that protest still going on back at the park?"

"Yes, Barb." The Police Chief looked like he'd aged ten years in as many minutes. "We closed the streets here by City Hall after that cape shot at us and the protesters went back to the park to carry on. I've got officers monitoring the situation but so far they're behaving."

"Who, the protesters or the officers?" Breezy challenged, arms crossed in front of him..

"Both." The Police Chief's face grew red and Annalisa knew Breezy had scored a low blow on him.

"I think the best thing we can do is to get the word out about the officers being arrested as soon as possible," Annalisa said. "Hopefully with them seeing some progress, the protesters will go home and then if Blindspot is here, he won't have anyone to go after."

"I agree," Aighleigh said. "Madam Mayor?"

Babcock pulled out her ponytail, shook out her hair, then tied it back once more. "God, I remember when the hardest thing I had to do was to convince people to vote for a tax increase to fix their roads. Robert . . . after we make the announcement about the arrests, I want to follow it up with a temporary ten o'clock curfew. Just for tonight. We'll make sure people know it's just for tonight, and it's for their safety. Knowing they've got at least one parahuman out there willing to attack a crowd will help that. We'll do a press conference tomorrow morning at nine o'clock and I hope to God we can figure out something to say that will bring an end to all this."

"It won't ever end, Madam Mayor," Jacob said. "One Mayor can't fix a broken system."

"Maybe not, young man," Babcock said. "But that doesn't mean I shouldn't try."

Annalisa and the others said goodbye to the adults and strode out of the room, feeling triumphant. And why shouldn't they? They'd gotten a bunch of adults—adults who had *clout*—to agree with them and it felt to Annalisa like things might finally turn around. The five kids headed down the hall, Aighleigh's footsteps clicking on the floor and echoing off the walls. When they were out of earshot of the conference room, they stopped for a moment to congratulate each other with smiles and high-fives.

"So what happens now?" Chloe asked.

"Are you and Jacob staying?" Annalisa asked. "You can spend the night at my house. You too, Aighleigh."

Chloe smiled. "A middle school slumber party? I haven't done one of those since I was in gymnastics. Sure, if it's okay with your folks."

"It will be," Annalisa said, making a mental note to sweeten the pot with some extra chores on Sunday if needed.

"I'll have to run home first," Aighleigh said. "Heh. I love saying that. But my batteries are getting low and I don't want to stall halfway between here and anywhere else."

"I can carry you if you're cool with it," Annalisa said. Normally she wouldn't offer, and Aighleigh wouldn't accept. She felt very strongly about doing things on her own without help, but there were times when practicality overrode pride.

"Yeah, that would be okay," Aighleigh said. "Then you ladies don't have to slow down for Little Miss Boston Dynamics."

Chloe laughed. "I bet you could engineer better legs than they could"

"You can crash at my place, Jacob," Breezy offered. "We got a spare room. It's got a bunch of junk in it in boxes, but at least it's got a bed."

"That sounds fine, Breezy. Thank you."

Breezy pulled out his phone, looked at it, sighed, and called his mom.

Annalisa, who hated talking on the phone when she could have been texting, knew exactly how he felt. At least her parents were a little more willing to answer a text than Breezy's mom.

Mama im bringn ayly & 1 more friend over 2 spend the nite ok?

After a minute, her mom replies, *That's fine.*

"Okay, we're cool with my folks," Annalisa said.

"My mom's good too," Breezy said.

"Hush, there's the Mayor," Aighleigh said, and then raised her voice to call to Babock. "Madam Mayor, do you need us to help enforce the curfew after you make your announcement?" Aighleigh asked. "We're willing and able."

"No, Wheels, I believe we have things in hand. I appreciate the offer, but I'd rather have you all present tomorrow morning at my press conference."

She left the next part unsaid, but Annalisa thought it just the same.

They'd probably be needed more then.

Chapter Twenty-Four

Breezy manned up enough to kiss Annalisa in front of everyone else before inflating his cape and flying off toward his house with Jacob trotting along beneath him. Chloe grinned at her as the two boys passed out of hearing range. "Well, he seems like quite the catch."

"He's my friend," Annalisa said. "We've known each other forever. We all have."

"We grew up together. Same schools and everything," Aighleigh added. "All our birthdays are in the same two weeks, even."

"Five of you, all basically the same age, in the same town? That's odd," Chloe said.

"Yeah, it is, and actually there were eight of us. The triplets moved to New York a couple years ago. Statistically, it's so unlikely that it can't be random chance. I've been investigating it in my copious spare time. You know, in between supervillains and riots and Calculus." Aighleigh checked a reading on her suit. "Yeah, right now I have just enough power to go three, maybe four blocks, and then I'm crawling. Annalisa, if you don't mind . . ."

Annalisa looked at the quadropede. "What's the best way to pick this thing up so I don't break it?"

Aighleigh popped open a hatch on the side of the rig's rear hips. "I planned for that. There are two straps in there, like what truckers use to tie down loads. Run them through the loops welded onto the flanks and belly and then you can just carry me like a big, centaur-shaped purse."

"Watch out for muggers," Chloe said.

Annalisa followed Aighleigh's instructions and got the straps properly connected to the quadropede. "You sure these are going to hold?"

"Yes, they're rated for a heck of a lot more weight than me. But I'm not worried about you dropping me. I'm way less heavy than a helicopter."

"I didn't catch the helicopter," Annalisa grumbled. Nevertheless, she pulled the straps over her shoulder and lifted a few feet off the ground by way of experiment. The rig swung beneath her, centering itself with its legs dangling. "How's that feel?"

"Like a mall parking lot amusement ride," Aighleigh said. "All it needs is a skeevy pothead at the controls."

Chloe laughed and lifted herself into the air. She flew above and behind the other two so as to keep the buzz of her wings from drowning out their conversation. As Annalisa flew, Aighleigh kept her nose firmly buried in her phone and reported on social media updates as they came across the feed. "Mayor just announced the arrest of the two officers. She's ordered the curfew and asked people to go home and be safe with their loved ones. I asked Vinnie to retweet everything. The word is out."

"What are other people saying?" Chloe asked.

"Oh, it's all over the place. Some people are saying it's a trick, or that the Mayor is flat out lying. You know, hashtag fake news and all that. Others are replying and thanking her for her

efforts to get justice for Dominic Ortega."
Aighleigh sighed. "A lot of people can't even spell
his name right. People are dumb. They just pile
onto social media because they want to be a part of
something bigger than themselves. Most of the
time, they don't even know what they're really
talking about."

"I know we're not supposed to enforce the
curfew . . ." Annalisa angled her flight in the
general direction of the park where she'd first
found Dominic Ortega's body. "But we do kind of
go right by that park on the way to your house. We
could still overfly it. You know, make sure
everyone is doing the right thing."

"Sounds like a good idea to me," Chloe said.
"Especially with Cernícala still out there and
maybe Blindspot."

"You know you can't see him," Annalisa said.
"Neither can you, Aighleigh."

"I can't figure out how something like that
works," Aighleigh said. "I hate stuff I can't figure out."

"I couldn't see the picture of him either," Chloe
said. "That means his power isn't just telepathic or
something. It's . . . I don't know what it is. I guess
that's up to people smarter than me."

"Maybe if you thought real hard about not
being white?" Annalisa suggested, only half joking.

"I'm from Idaho," Chloe said. "They don't come
much whiter than that."

They flew over the park, high enough they'd be
hard to spot in the darkness. Chloe adjusted her wings
to stealth mode. There was still a group of protesters,
but they seemed far less agitated than they had been
in earlier gatherings. Many were strolling away from
the park, perhaps heading back to their cars or home

for the night. Those who remained were peaceful, talking amongst themselves instead of chanting or shouting. The police officers monitoring the situation weren't just standing back at arm's length with their riot gear. Instead, they spoke with the protesters.

"It worked," Annalisa said softly. "Look, they're actually talking."

"We don't know that it worked," Aighleigh said. "But you're right. Maybe the Mayor has this figured out. I suppose there are some politicians who aren't morons."

Chloe snorted. "Heh. You're still young."

"What are you, three, four years older than us?"

Annalisa snickered at the banter as she descended toward the Neighborhood Watch headquarters. Chloe followed her and a moment later, all three girls were on solid ground. Aighleigh trotted across the yard to her storage container and emerged in a few minutes in her wheelchair once more with a duffel bag in her lap. "Okay, I'm ready. Let's fly."

Chloe's stomach rumbled loud enough for Annalisa to pause, wondering if something was wrong with her. The towheaded girl blushed hard enough for Annalisa to see it even in the glow of the streetlights illuminating the salvage yard. "Uh . . . You guys hungry at all? Flying uses a lot of calories." She patted a pouch on her costume. "My treat."

Aighleigh grinned. "You like burgers?"

"Never met one I couldn't get outside of."

A few minutes later and the three young heroes emerged from the Good Times Burgers, laden with four five-packs of sliders and a double order of large fries. Chloe crammed half of one of the greasy sandwiches into her mouth and wiped dressing from the corner of her lips. She closed her eyes and chewed in gustatory bliss.

"You need a minute or two alone?" Annalisa asked.

Chloe swallowed and smiled. "This is really good. I think I could eat ten or fifteen of these myself."

Aighleigh handed her a bag with nine sandwiches in it. "Go crazy. I couldn't eat like that. I'd weigh three hundred pounds. I guess my powers don't work that way."

"Mine do, kind of," Annalisa said. "Let me get some fries before the human dragonfly discovers how good they are."

Aighleigh raised a couple fries up toward Annalisa's mouth, since Annalisa's hands were otherwise occupied in keeping her from falling. They flew along like that, Aighleigh feeding her friend like she was giving treats to an animal. Annalisa couldn't help giggling at that and soon all three girls were chuckling as they flew over the neighborhoods to Annalisa's house.

They landed in the back yard, Chloe being careful to modulate her wings so as not to disturb the neighbors. True to her prediction, she'd inhaled ten sliders and gave an unladylike belch as she touched down to the ground. She belatedly covered her mouth and whispered, "Sorry!"

Annalisa opened the back door into the kitchen. She could hear the TV on in the living room. "Mamá, Papi, we're here."

Her parents appeared at the kitchen door a moment later. Her mom rushed over to embrace her. "I'm so glad you're home, *hija*. You too, Aighleigh." She bent to hug Aighleigh in her chair. "We were watching the news. They had a feature on you and the pilot you saved today."

"Did you change your costume?" her father asked.

"Oh . . . yeah. Mamá, Papi, this is WyldWing. She's with Just Cause. She's going to help us track down the supervillain who attacked the protest today. She also got me this new costume because mine was all tore up."

Chloe peeled off her gloves and extended a hand to Annalisa's parents. "Call me Chloe, Mr. and Mrs. Torres. Thank you for letting me stay here."

"Nonsense. Any friend of Annalisa's is welcome here anytime," Annalisa's mom said.

"*Nuestra casa es su casa*," her father said.

"That means our house is your house," Annalisa said.

"Do you need anything to drink?" Annalisa's mom eyed the bags of sliders and fries, mostly empty after the girls' ravenous mid-air feast. "We've got tea, Coke, lemonade . . ."

The girls settled on some Mexican Cokes and went to Annalisa's room. She slid out the trundle bed from beneath hers so they'd all have room to sit and stretch out. Aighleigh flopped out of her chair and passed it to Annalisa to fold up for her. She pulled herself across the mattress, dragging the dead weight of her legs, until she flipped over and rested her back against Annalisa's bed.

"You mind if I change?" Chloe asked.

"Into what?" Aighleigh asked. "Do you transform or something?"

Chloe laughed. "No, but I'm ready to be out of this costume." She produced something like a tightly-folded gymnastics leotard from another pouch and undid the fasteners on her costume. Annalisa had never considered the mechanics of how clothing had to work for a winged body, and found the process interesting. Beneath her costume, Chloe wore a sports bra and athletic shorts. Her body was taut with well-defined athletic musculature. Her leotard had a deep-cut back, allowing her wings to remain unfettered.

"You've got a lot of extra muscles in your back," Aighleigh said. "I can see them. I guess your wings must need them, huh?"

Chloe nodded. "Yeah, they had to give some of them new names, because they don't exist in any other human. I'm unique in the catalog of human physiology."

"How do you sleep?" Annalisa asked. "I mean, do you have to sleep on your stomach?"

"Yeah, I had to get used to that. Sometimes I still roll over in my sleep and crush them."

Aighleigh winced in sympathy. "Does that hurt? I bet it hurts."

Chloe shook her head. "No, it's uncomfortable, but not any more so than when you sleep on your arm wrong and your hand falls asleep. Mostly it just looks terrible. You think bedhead is bad? You should see *bedwings*. I look like a piece of crumpled plastic wrap."

The girls laughed and drank their Cokes. Annalisa got out of her new costume, almost sad to do so. "I really like it," she said, folding it and setting it on the foot of her bed. "Thank you again, Chloe."

Chloe nodded. "No problem. I'm glad to help."

Annalisa and Aighleigh arranged themselves on Annalisa's bed so Chloe would have the trundle bed to herself. "It's really not necessary," Chloe said. "I'll be fine with a corner."

"Nonsense," Aighleigh said, sounding just like Annalisa's mom. "I don't move in my sleep. What am

I going to do, kick you?" She smiled. "And Annalisa can hover in her sleep. I've seen her do it."

"I *what*?" Annalisa's mouth dropped open in shock.

Aighleigh giggled. "I should have taken a picture. Last time I was here, when I woke up in the middle of the night, you were floating two feet over your bed."

"Sleep-flying," Chloe said. "That's hysterical."

"That's terrifying," Annalisa said. "What if I, you know, flew out the window or something?"

"You're bulletproof, you'll be fine," Aighleigh said. "I guess you could always tether yourself."

"What, like a . . . a leash?"

"Even something you just put around your ankle. Something that would tug you awake if you started to drift away," Aighleigh said. "Put the other end around your bed. You're strong, but you're not going to pull your entire bed through the wall in your sleep."

Annalisa yawned. "I'm tired enough, I might try anyway."

Chloe set her phone on the floor beside her. "I set an alarm so we have plenty of time to make the Mayor's press conference in the morning."

"And after that, we go find Cernícala," Aighleigh said. "And Blindspot if he's here."

Aighleigh checked her own phone. "Vinnie's still on the bench, but Cole says he'll be there tomorrow too."

Annalisa texted Breezy. *U guys comin tmrw rite?*

Breezy responded almost immediately with a thumbs-up emoji. Then . . . *we playin CoD.*

Annalisa rolled her eyes. Call of Duty. "Boys."

Chapter Twenty-Five

Saturday, May 9, 2020
Loveland, CO

Annalisa's dad made chilaquiles again for the girls for breakfast. Chloe had never had such a dish and she ate two platefuls of the fried tortillas with eggs, bacon, and green chile. "This is amazing, Mr. Torres," she said in between mouthfuls. "I'm never having a breakfast burrito again."

"Please, call me Omar, Chloe," said Annalisa's dad, who nevertheless looked pleased at the praise.

"Coffee?" Annalisa's mom asked.

"Yes, please, and thank you." Chloe held out her cup.

"Can I have some too?" Annalisa asked. If coffee was what *real* superheroes drank, then she would drink it too.

Annalisa's mom raised an eyebrow. "Really? Last time you tried it you said it tasted like dirt."

"Mom, I was just a kid then."

"You're a kid now, *hija.*"

"Can I just have some coffee, please?"

Annalisa's mom shrugged and poured out a mug for Annalisa. Annalisa sniffed at the steam and tried not to wrinkle her nose. "Mmmm . . ." she said, closing her eyes and inhaling deeply.

Aighleigh chuckled as she watched Annalisa pour probably way too much sugar into the cup, followed by a generous dollop of milk. "I figured you'd like your coffee like you like your men, Annalisa. Black and strong."

Annalisa faked a scandalized gasp. "I like it sweet."

Chloe sipped her own coffee. "Me too."

Even with the sugar and milk helping to tame the flavor, coffee was still coffee and Annalisa had to make herself drink it. It helped that Chloe drank hers without any change of expression.

The girls finished breakfast and took their plates to the kitchen. Annalisa's mom reminded her that she needed to unload the dishwasher after she came back from the Mayor's press conference. Annalisa grimaced at being reminded of her chores in front of her friends, but nodded.

"Do you have a costume we need to go get?" Chloe asked Aighleigh as she and Annalisa changed. After confirming it was safe to do so, Annalisa's mom had machine-washed hers and Annalisa's costumes so they smelled clean and fresh.

"I don't have a costume," Aighleigh said. "I mean, what's the point? I still have to either ride a chair or the quadropede. I've been emailing back and forth with a couple of researchers at Boston Dynamics. They talk to me like I'm an adult, which is pretty cool. They helped me with building the legs I have now. I think they want me to come work there. They're all giddy about maybe having a technopath on their team."

"Would you do that instead of being on Just Cause?" Chloe asked as she wriggled her wings through the slots in the back of her suit.

"Maybe I could do both."

"If anybody can pull that off, it's you." Annalisa adjusted her cape.

"You know, there's some old Destroyer tech in the Just Cause archives in Denver. I wonder if you could do anything with it," Chloe mused. "It's just gathering dust. I bet you could use it. It's like a horse. A robot horse."

Aighleigh's eyebrows nearly shot up above her hairline. "Destroyer built a *robotic horse*? That sounds amazing. Can I admit something? I always wished I could have met him."

"He was a supervillain," Annalisa pointed out.

"Yeah, but he was a technomancer like me. I bet we'd have had a lot to talk about."

"I bet he'd have tried to kill you," Annalisa said.

Aighleigh shrugged. "Maybe, maybe not. We'll never know now. Still, robot horse, am I right?"

"You couldn't call yourself Wheels anymore," Annalisa said as she pulled on her boots.

"Cavalier," Aighleigh said immediately.

"What's that?"

"It's an ancient warrior. Like part of the cavalry."

"Oooh, I like that," Annalisa said. "You could make tech armor and a tech sword and a tech, uh, bow and arrows and stuff. Get the whole knight thing going." She could almost see the wheels turning in her friend's mind as ideas flooded thick and fast.

"Yeah . . ." Aighleigh's voice was far away.

Annalisa snapped in front of her friend's face. "Earth to Aighleigh. Invent later. We're going to be late if we don't get going. Do you want the chair today or your quadro-thingie?"

"Quadropede," Aighleigh said. "Sorry." She turned to Chloe. "When I get an idea like this, it's like the blueprints just draw themselves in my mind. I can already see how to build the thing. I did my current setup *all wrong*. I'll have to tear it apart and start over."

"I'm sorry," Chloe said.

"No, it's good. I'm excited about it."

Annalisa texted Breezy. *Meet us @ hq n well go together.*

Ok, he replied right away.

"You guys ready?" Aighleigh gave her a thumbs-up and snapped the safety belt of her wheelchair shut.

"Good to go." Chloe pulled her goggles down over her face.

Annalisa wheeled Aighleigh down the hall while her friend secured her bag so it wouldn't slip out of her lap. "Mamá, we're leaving."

"Okay, *hija*. Be careful. You too, Aighleigh and WyldWing."

"Chloe, ma'am. Friends get to call me by my name." Chloe smiled.

"Then I'm Sara."

"Thanks for having me over, Sara."

"You're welcome anytime, Chloe." Annalisa's mom checked her phone. "You girls better hurry."

Annalisa rolled Aighleigh out the door with Chloe right behind her. "Don't worry. We can fly fast."

She slipped the straps over her shoulders and lifted Aighleigh's chair into the sky.

* * *

The Neighborhood Watch was in full attendance at the Mayor's press conference. Even Vinnie had managed to convince his mom to let him attend, although he wasn't his usual boisterous self. He wore his regular costume along with the devil mask, and a Colorado Eagles baseball hat over it with the brim pulled down low to shield his eyes from the morning sun. He had climbed up the brick front of the building and sat on the overhang of the second floor, his legs dangling over the edge. Breezy perched opposite Vinnie, enshrouded in his voluminous blue cloak. He, too, had added a baseball hat to his costume, with the icon of a raised black fist on a white field prominently displayed. Annalisa wondered if that might be too overtly political, but then decided the heroes were under no obligation to maintain a sense of neutrality, so long as they didn't play favorites when it came to doing their jobs.

Doing their jobs.

Deep down, Annalisa knew that what they were doing, providing a visible presence and security for the Mayor's press conference most definitely was *not* their job. They were a bunch of fourteen-year-olds with no business doing anything on a Saturday morning except sleeping in or getting ready for some serious weekending. They were there pretty much only at the Mayor's pleasure, and if she told them they were no longer welcome, they would have to leave.

The best thing they could do, Aighleigh said, was make sure they were out of the way and unobtrusive as possible without actually being invisible. "If Cernícala or Blindspot shows up, we want them to know we're here." She'd been the one to assign locations, along with Chloe and Jacob.

Cole, Jacob, and Aighleigh were placed near the steps in strategic locations where they could watch the sky and the crowd gathering to hear the Mayor's conference, just like Vinnie and Breezy could look out over the crowd and get a bird's eye view. Annalisa and Chloe hovered over the onlookers where they could keep an eye on the Mayor, the other officials, and the police. Aighleigh's hope was that by splitting the group someone would see Blindspot if he showed up, and Cernícala would have a tough time approaching unseen as well. It was the best they could do with the resources they had, Aighleigh said, and Annalisa had agreed.

Chloe and Jacob had likewise deferred to Aighleigh's leadership, which spoke a lot about their willingness to integrate with a team and not be glory hounds. "Are you sure you're okay to hover for a long time?" Annalisa asked Chloe. "I mean, you fly differently than I do. As long as I'm not actually doing anything but hovering, it's not any harder than standing. But you're using muscles."

Chloe smiled. "I'm good to fly for hours and hours," she said. "And if worst comes to worst, I've got snacks." She held up a wrapped bar for evidence. "There's a place in Boulder that makes these special for parahumans. They're packed with calories and nutrients for those of us who burn hotter and harder than normal humans."

Annalisa laughed. "You sound like a commercial."

Chloe cleared her throat. "Well, uh, they might want me to be a spokesperson."

Annalisa gaped at Chloe. "For real? Like, a what-do-you-call-it?"

"An endorsement deal," Aighleigh said over her earpiece. "Like an athlete selling shoes or an actor selling yogurt that makes you poop better."

Everyone laughed.

"Is that a thing that happens when you're in Just Cause?"

"Sometimes, I guess," Chloe said. "You know, Mustang Sally once endorsed Ford, back when she beat the speed of sound."

"I think I remember seeing a special on that," Hothead said. "It was at that place where they do all the jet cars and stuff."

Annalisa wondered if anyone would ever want her to endorse anything. If they did, would she say yes? She wanted to ask how much Chloe was getting paid, but thought better of it. Her parents made a decent living for the three of them between her father's construction and her mother's office work. As far as Annalisa knew, they'd never been in a really risky financial situation, but she didn't know if her folks would have ever said anything to her if they had. Still, it would be awesome to buy them something nice—something they'd never had, like a brand new truck for her dad or a redone kitchen for her mom, or a vacation for both of them.

First things first, Annalisa, she told herself. It wasn't like ad executives were backing up a dump truck full of cash to her door.

The Mayor began her conference with a speech. Annalisa tried to listen but her attention wandered quickly as it sounded like almost every other political speech she'd ever heard. She swept her gaze slowly across the crowd below, wondering if Cernícala was hiding among the gathered people. They weren't protesting—not really. A few people were carrying signs but most were there to listen to the Mayor after her announcement of the arrests of the two officers who'd shot Dominic Ortega. They wanted to know what was going to happen next, what charges were going to be filed, and what the city was going to do to make sure it didn't happen again.

That's when Annalisa saw the police officer with the rifle walking behind the others lined up along the steps.

Chapter Twenty-Six

It struck Annalisa as odd right away, seeing a police officer with a weapon when none of the others had any weapons out at all. They had their pistols and tasers, of course, but they were all holstered. Why the rifle?

And then she knew.

"Chloe, you see that cop in the back? The one with the rifle?"

"Where?" Chloe raised her goggles as if they were making it harder to see.

Annalisa was already on the move. "It's him! Blindspot!" She raced over the crowd toward the man with the rifle. "Gun! Gun!" she screamed.

Jacob moved with a speedster's reflexes, wrapping his arms around Mayor Babcock and bearing her to the ground, careful to keep her from bouncing her head off the cement steps in front of City Hall.

"Where is he?" Aighleigh cried.

With a flapping of fabric, Breezy inflated his cape and flew off his perch, already blasting a mostly-ineffectual downdraft toward the rifleman. Blindspot raised his rifle toward the crowd of onlookers. Enough of them could see him that they screamed in panic. They turned to flee, fighting past each other and trampling those who weren't quick or nimble enough to get out of the way.

Just as Blindspot pulled the trigger, Annalisa crashed into his field of fire. Bullets smashed into her, each one feeling like a punch to the guts. Other police officers drew their pistols, trying to see where the shots were coming from.

Officers Bickle and Velez could both see Blindspot. "Freeze!" Bickle bellowed as he and his partner drew their weapons.

Blindspot touched something clipped to his bulletproof vest and then it seemed like the whole world exploded into flashes of fire and smoke and thunder. Several trash cans around the plaza erupted, adding to the chaos and making Bickle and Velez dive to safety as one near them went up, peppering them with shrapnel and flaming debris. Aighleigh shrieked as a whirling piece of metal took out one of her quadropede's legs and she fell sideways. Cole's entire head ignited like a torch as he ran to her.

Annalisa realized she was still standing after being shot a half dozen times and having a trash can explode near her. Her ears were ringing from the explosions but her head was clear, and she saw Blindspot drop his rifle and run into City Hall. "I'm —I'm going after him," she said, not knowing if any of her teammates could hear her.

"I'll come too," said Jacob. "I saw him."

"No, you're not bulletproof." Annalisa threw open the door. "Help anyone who's hurt. Get the fires out. Watch out for Cernícala."

She plunged into the City Hall interior and a bullet smashed into her shoulder, gunfire thundering in her ears. "Damn it!"

Blindspot sprinted down the hall to the exit doors at the far end. He spun and fired again, using a pistol this time. Annalisa barely dodged. She'd already decided that, bulletproof or not, being shot hurt and she would do her best to stay out of his line of fire if she could. He shouldered through the doors and she flew after him, hoping to catch him before he made his escape. In a split second, she decided not to stop since there wasn't anybody immediately beyond the glass doors, putting her fists ahead of her as she approached the far end of the hall.

With a crash, she burst through the glass, barely feeling the impact. The steel door frames bent like cotton candy with the force of her blasting through them. She saw Blindspot commandeering a vehicle, forcing a terrified young man out at gunpoint. As the civilian screamed in fear, Blindspot turned and flung something to the ground before jumping into the car. Annalisa gasped, seeing wires and flashing LEDs and the fallen civilian right beside it.

She didn't know if being bulletproof extended to being bombproof, but she had no time to worry about it. She raced across the cement plaza at City Hall's rear entrance and swept up the device in passing. What should she do with a bomb that could explode at any moment? Inspiration struck, and she spun herself around once like an Olympic hammer thrower. The bomb went sailing into the sky to explode harmlessly a couple seconds later, doing nothing worse than startling a handful of birds.

Blindspot's stolen car, something black and low to the ground with a loud engine, roared out of the lot and ran the stop sign at the end of the block. Tires screeched as a couple cars crossing slammed on their brakes to avoid the fleeing supervillain.

Annalisa paused long enough to ask the man at her feet if he was all right. He stammered that he was. "Stay here," Annalisa said. "Help is on the way."

She hurtled after Blindspot.

Horns blared as Blindspot ran a red light, narrowly missing getting broadsided by a pickup truck. The truck hit the median and nearly crossed into incoming traffic before jouncing to a stop, straddling the traffic island. Annalisa grimaced as she sped past. If Blindspot caused a bad accident, she might have to let him go to help victims. She heard the shriek of distant sirens as emergency vehicles responded to the mayhem Blindspot had caused at City Hall.

Ahead of her, Blindspot skidded sideways into an intersection in a screeching left turn. As he did so, he hung one hand out the window and fired three shots at Annalisa. None of them struck her but she still ducked out of reflex. It occurred to her that the bullets would still come down eventually, and could hurt someone . . . or worse.

She'd make a point of letting the next burst hit her instead, no matter how much it hurt.

The black car accelerated like a dragster on its new course, heading west toward the mountains. Maybe he was going to try to lose her in the canyon. She didn't think that would work—she didn't have to worry about running off the road like he did, but she could already tell his stolen car was faster than her top flight speed, and black cars were so common that if she lost sight of him for more than a few seconds, he might get away altogether.

He roared through another intersection and this time, two cars collided as they both jerked in the same direction to avoid colliding with the fleeing supervillain. Annalisa clenched her jaw and kept going. The car was pulling further and further away from her and Blindspot knew he was getting away.

Half the noise raging in her head was from her earpiece, and she hadn't been able to make heads or tails what was happening back at City Hall. "Aighleigh, Chloe, anyone. I'm in pursuit of Blindspot. He's in a stolen black car. I don't know what kind it is. He's heading west."

"We're all okay," Aighleigh said. "People got hurt by the exploding trash cans, but nobody's going to die."

Annalisa yelped in surprise as Blindspot crossed the center line to avoid cars stopped at a light. Sparks shot from the undercarriage of the car as he jumped a curb to avoid the cars facing the opposite direction. Annalisa held her breath, half hoping he would wipe out right then, half afraid he would do exactly that. Somehow, he saved it, and fishtailed back onto the street again.

Behind her, Annalisa heard approaching sirens and risked a glance back. A pair of police cars were tearing up the road after Blindspot. One was a silver State Patrol car, the kind of low-slung, speedy-looking sedan that was probably all engine, and a white SUV from Loveland Police Department.

Annalisa ducked as she nearly flew right into a power line crossing the road. She made herself gain altitude even though it slowed her down. She could see Blindspot's car better from the higher vantage point, but the only way she could even tell which black car was his was that he was going twice as fast as everyone else.

She poured on the speed, desperate to eke out even a fraction more just to keep the car in her sight before he vanished into the distance.

"Aighleigh, point me in the right direction." That was Jacob's voice over the comms. Was he coming to help? He was a speedster, and a world-class one at that. Even if he wasn't bulletproof, he could at least be Annalisa's eyes on the ground when she couldn't keep up with Blindspot.

"She's heading west on Eisenhower."

"No idea where that is, but I know which way is west."

Annalisa pulled out her phone, opened the map, and dropped a pin on it. "This road, Jacob. Hurry, he's driving faster than I can fly." She shared the link to the Neighborhood Watch app, then tucked the phone into the pouch built into her costume's hip.

Ahead, a Larimer County sheriff's cruiser swerved out in front of Blindspot's car, trying to box him in. Brake lights flashed and suddenly Annalisa was gaining on the fleeing supervillain. He skidded over a curb and caught the corner of a parked car. Pieces of body panels flew in all directions as he roared into a dirt parking lot. A great cloud of dust swirled into the sky as he floored the accelerator. Pebbles flew like bullets as the car swayed left and right, seeking traction.

Annalisa narrowed her eyes into slits and pressed her lips together so she wouldn't accidentally inhale a lungful of dirt as she dove toward Blindspot. She slammed her shoulder into the car's rear quarter panel, spinning it around in the dust. She caught a momentary glimpse of the shocked expression on Blindspot's face before he dropped something dark out the window.

The explosion caught Annalisa in the side, throwing her through the air to crash into the

Loveland SUV. The impact drove the air from her lungs and snapped her head around like it was on the end of a string. The SUV spun crazily like it had hit a patch of black ice and went sideways into the ditch at the edge of the parking lot, shedding its light bar and one wheel in the process.

For a moment, Annalisa didn't dare move. She was stuck halfway into the back seat of the SUV, having smashed into the rear door hard enough to stave it in like she'd been a hammer and it an anvil. She tasted blood and wondered if she'd bitten her tongue. Her ears rang like she'd been listening to too much loud music for too long. She yanked herself free from the wreckage. The officer behind the wheel struggled with her seat belt. The impact had triggered the airbags and they hung around her like weird membranes.

"Are you okay?" Annalisa felt like she was shouting but could barely hear herself.

"Y-yeah," the officer said. "I . . . can't get out."

"Holy shit, Annalisa!" Jacob skidded to a halt on the street, staggering and dancing as he shed his velocity. "Are you all right?"

The SUV door was still hanging off her forearm. She shook it free. "I'm okay, Jacob."

Police cars flashed passed, sirens howling. Another couple screeched to a halt and the officers ran over to help.

Annalisa tore aside the driver's side door and glanced at Jacob. "Go after him. You can see him. He's driving a black car."

"What kind of car is it?"

Annalisa snapped the seat belt latch and helped the officer from her car. She staggered and Annalisa had to support her until the other police officers took over. "I don't know. It's black. But it's probably the only one trying to outrun the police. And it's pretty damaged." She looked through the clearing dust to the west. "He's going to have to slow down. The road gets twisty in the canyon. Be careful. He's got bombs and guns."

"Are you sure you're okay? You look . . ."

"Like I got blown up. Yeah." Annalisa shook her head to clear it. She clenched her fists. Blindspot was not going to get the best of her. Not today. Not after everything. "Go. I'm right behind you."

Jacob disappeared in a blur of motion, leaving behind another swirling cloud of dust.

The officer who had wrecked in the ditch leaned on the hood of another police car, her fellow officers keeping her upright. She raised a shaky hand to Annalisa. "Go get that son of a bitch, Capitána, whoever he is."

Annalisa nodded and felt her cape tighten around her shoulders as she launched herself into the sky like an angry red and green missile.

Blindspot was going to pay.

Chapter Twenty-Seven

Aighleigh had planned ahead, as so many geniuses tended to, and given the Neighborhood Watch not two but three different channels upon which they could communicate through the app. Although the young superheroes hadn't had any situations thus far where they'd needed multiple lines of communications, the chatter of the others on the main frequency was distracting Annalisa. "Hey, Jacob, switch your app to comm channel B."

"Yipe!" he shouted, nearly blowing Annalisa's earbud right out of her ear. "Sorry . . . took a corner too wide an' nearly pancaked myself on a truck."

"Aighleigh, have everyone else switch to channel B. Jacob doesn't need the distraction."

The noise from the rest of the Watch back at City Hall ended as the team gave the primary channel over for Annalisa's and Jacob's exclusive use.

"That's better," she said. The canyon walls rose around her as she raced after the fleeing Blindspot. The road dropped to two lanes, which meant he was at risk of getting stuck behind a slower vehicle with too much oncoming traffic to pass. "Jacob, you got him in sight?" She ducked under a pipeline that crossed over the road. Somewhere behind her, a driver beeped his or her horn twice.

"Think so. There always this much traffic in y'all's hills?"

"It's the beginning of summer. People are going camping." Annalisa flew over a camper chugging up the hill as she spoke. The river burbled down to her right and a fresh breeze blew down the canyon, carrying a delicate hint of mountain wildflowers with overtones of diesel exhaust.

"I got him! Four cars up. He's weavin' in and out."

Just as Jacob announced it, Annalisa rounded the bend and saw the orange figure of the speedster likewise weaving in and out of traffic, and up ahead was that suspicious black car.

Annalisa ducked away from the road to fly low over the river where she would neither be a distraction to drivers nor at risk of running into a car coming the opposite direction.

The black car passed another car on the right, scraping along the jersey barriers in a shower of sparks. Horns blared and tires squealed as the car skidded around a tight S-curve. Annalisa saw Jacob go sliding off the road to the left on his hip, scattering dirt as he came to a stop against the canyon wall. "Jacob!" she cried.

"I'm all right," he said, sounding like he was spitting out a mouthful of gravel. "Get him before he hurts someone else."

Blindspot fishtailed around another curve, catching the rear panel of an oncoming sedan with the corner of his front bumper. Bodywork shattered and the car coming downhill skidded to a halt, nearly getting broadsided by a truck behind it. The black car started pulling away once more now that it was through the most dangerous twists in the road.

Annalisa flew up and over the guardrail, staying low behind Blindspot's car. As soon as she saw a big enough break in the oncoming traffic, she acted. Shooting forward like she'd found a higher gear, she pulled alongside the black car and leaned her shoulder against the driver's side door.

Blindspot shouted in surprise as his stolen car bounced off the guard rail. He jerked the wheel over to bash the car against Annalisa, trying to swat her into an oncoming RV like an insect.

She didn't give him any space, and shoved the car over a lot harder than she had before. The car hit the guardrail again and its left-side wheels came off the ground. In a flash, Annalisa dove beneath it. She hadn't done much crawling around under cars and didn't know to expect. She grabbed the first thing she thought looked solid and heaved.

Once, when she was younger, Annalisa had lifted the back end of an armored truck off the ground to keep a would-be thief from getting away. She'd looked it up later. It had probably weighed more than twelve tons. No wonder she hadn't done much more than raise it a couple inches. She was older now, and stronger, and Blindspot's car was much lighter than an armored truck.

It flipped up and over the guard rail, the sudden howl of the revving engine drowning out Blindspot's scream. Annalisa realized belatedly she had gone too far and went over the guardrail after the tumbling car. She wasn't fast enough to stop its fall and it crashed into the river on the passenger side. Airbags flared white inside the cabin for a moment before deflating as the car's momentum made it roll over onto its roof. The river wasn't deep enough for the car to sink, but it was deep enough for water to fill the overturned cabin halfway up the doors.

Annalisa knew she had only seconds to act. She dropped into the raging current, braced herself against the rocks, and pushed against the car's door frame. It felt like she wasn't just trying to lift the car alone, but the entire river along with it. For all she knew, the way the water had filled the cabin, she might have been doing exactly that. Nevertheless, she heaved and strained until with a creaking of stressed body panels, the car tipped onto its ruined passenger side. She shoved again and it tipped once more onto its wheels.

Water slopped out through the dented door. Inside, Blindspot hung from his seat belt like a rag doll, boneless. Annalisa wondered if she'd accidentally killed him. The thought made her stomach twist and she clenched her teeth to keep from puking. She could feel eyes on her as people had pulled over on the highway and watched from the road. River water had soaked through her costume and she was sopping wet from head to toe.

She tried to pull open the driver's side door but it was stuck thanks to the damage from rolling. She placed one hand on the door frame and the other on the door and pulled. For several long seconds, nothing happened as she pulled harder and harder. She heard a pinging sound as a piece of metal in the latch sheared away, and she tore the door open. For the first time, she got a good look at Blindspot.

She couldn't tell how old he was. His short buzz cut was blonde, as was the stubble decorating his cheeks and chin. The crown-of-thorns tattoo stood out sharp against his pale skin. Blood oozed from a long gash across his forehead, maybe from the airbag. His eyes were shut. Up close, she could see his police uniform looked like a costume shop rental, made from cheap material with *City Police Department* stitched on the shoulders. His guns and explosives were nowhere to be seen. Perhaps they'd fallen out when she'd flipped the car. No matter, she thought. He wasn't going to be using them.

Steeling herself for the worst, she stripped off a glove and reached out a shaking hand to touch his neck. She wasn't even sure what she was supposed to look for, but she'd seen everybody do it on TV, so she assumed it would be obvious if he was alive or not. She couldn't feel anything except his skin, clammy from the river water, but he stirred a little and moaned at her touch.

Annalisa sighed in relief. She hadn't killed him. Maybe it wouldn't have been the worst thing to happen to a supervillain, but she didn't want to face that stigma forever. She released his seat belt clasp and hauled him out of the car. He groaned louder. What if she was doing more injury to him by moving him? She'd heard it was dangerous to move someone who'd been in an accident.

Then she realized the truth was she simply didn't care. He'd gone to City Hall with the intent to injure and kill others. He was going to pay for his crimes, both in pain and in a court of law.

"Wh-what . . ." he began.

Annalisa spun him around so she was holding him from behind. She twisted one of his arms behind him and whispered in his ear. "Don't resist or I'll break your arm . . . Blindspot."

He slumped. "Goddammit," he whispered.

Annalisa smiled. "You got taken down by a *latina chica, cabrón*. I bet that really chaps your butt, huh?"

"Annalisa! You got him!" Jacob called from the road where he was watching along with the civilians and police who'd stopped.

"Got who? What's he talking about?" one of the officers called.

"That dude she's holding," said a man with dark skin. "Dumbass nearly ran me off the road."

Annalisa lifted herself and Blindspot out of the river. He didn't seem to have any weapons left on him but she shook him a bit just the same. "Try anything and I'll throw you against the canyon wall until everything is broken. Understand?"

"Y-yes."

Annalisa shivered. She'd never really threatened anyone before. It felt weird, like she was doing something wrong but delightful all the same. She reminded herself that she was holding a very bad man who was wanted for multiple assaults, attempted murder, and more, just in the short time he'd been in town. She landed on the roadside and looked around at the onlookers until she saw a police officer who wasn't white, and approached him. "This man is a supervillain called Blindspot. He's invisible to white people, but you can see him, can't you?"

The officer was a Larimer County deputy. His badge said Gavriel. He nodded.

"He's the one who shot at people and set off the bombs at City Hall this morning. Arrest him."

"Are you sure?" Deputy Gavriel asked.

"Officer, I'm Calamity, from Just Cause," Jacob said. "I will testify to that. La Capitána caught him. He's a wanted criminal. Book his ass."

The three officers present discussed it among themselves. Two were county deputies and one was from Loveland. They agreed that Blindspot was partially invisible, as only Deputy Gavriel could see him. At the very least, it made him a danger, and when they ran the plates on the car in the river, thanks to Annalisa retrieving one, they agreed he had stolen it. That was good enough for them, and they advised Blindspot of his rights, thoroughly searched him for more weapons, and after they were satisfied he had none, put him in the back of the deputy's car.

"You want a ride back into town?" Gavriel asked Annalisa and Jacob. "I've got room for one of you."

"No, I'll run. I'm good," Jacob said.

"If, uh, you don't mind," Annalisa said. "Can I come watch you book him in? He's a supervillain, and he's dangerous. Someone who can see him needs to keep an eye on him until he's behind bars."

"You want to perp walk your collar?" Gavriel laughed. "By all means, young lady. After what you went through to catch him, I think you've earned it."

Annalisa sat gratefully in the passenger seat of Gavriel's cruiser. She was exhausted. Between her flight and her struggles with Blindspot and his stolen car, she felt like she could have napped for a week. "What's a perp walk like?"

Gavriel smiled, then looked back over his shoulder at Blindspot, handcuffed and stuck in the back seat. "It's the best."

Annalisa checked her phone. It was supposed to be waterproof but she doubted that the makers had rivers and superheroics in mind when they'd made it. Nevertheless, the screen turned on when she unlocked it and she saw multiple messages from Aighleigh, Breezy, and the rest of the Watch.

She switched her comm over to channel B. "This is La Capitána," she said. "I got Blindspot. We're bringing him in."

Chapter Twenty-Eight

News traveled fast in the age of social media, and by the time officer Gavriel pulled his cruiser up to the police station, a crowd had gathered. People had their phones out to take pictures, shoot video, and a couple people had actual cameras. Annalisa wondered if they were *real* journalists instead of opportunistic fans. "Wow," she said as she took in the crowd. "That's a lot of people."

"You're a hero, Capitána. You're *our* hero," Gavriel said as he put the cruiser into park.

Blindspot muttered something offensive.

"Another word from you and I'm going to let this young lady bounce your face off the pavement a couple times," Gavriel said.

"Go back to Mexico, you stupid pig." Blindspot's face was already bruised from the collision, and the cut on his forehead was still oozing blood. Annalisa had asked if they were supposed to take him to a hospital first. Gavriel said no, he was too dangerous and besides, the jail medic would look him over anyway.

"You look like hell already, *cabrón.* I don't think anybody would notice another bruise or broken face at this point." Gavriel glanced at Annalisa. "You want a few minutes alone with him? You're not a cop. You don't have the same rules to follow that we do. Accidents happen."

For an eternity, Annalisa considered whether or not to say yes. She could take him. Use her strength on him. Punish him for his crimes. Leave him broken and bloodied on the floor.

She could even kill him, the way he'd killed other people.

That last thought frightened her. That was the way parahumans became supervillains. That led to a dark place from which there was no returning.

"No . . ." she whispered. "That's not who I am."

"No sweat. I was just talking," Gavriel said. "You ready to show this loser off to the people?"

Annalisa turned on her selfie camera and frowned. Her face was muddy and her hair was sticking out in all directions from her dousing in the river. "I'm a mess."

"You look like a hero," Gavriel said. "Like you worked for it. Come on. Let's give the people what they want to see." He opened his door.

Annalisa opened hers and the crowd *cheered* as she stepped out. Cheered, like she was a rock star or something. "Capitána! Capitána!" they chanted.

Gavriel motioned for her to come around to the back door of the cruiser. He opened the door and stepped back. Annalisa realized he wanted her to take Blindspot from his seat. He snarled and spat at her.

"That's assault, *pendejo*," Gavriel said. "You got any kind of illness, it's attempted murder, now behave yourself before I forget my cheerful disposition." He nodded at Annalisa.

She looked over at the crowd. There were civilians and police cheering for her. White faces. Black faces. Brown faces. Without even meaning to, she'd found a way to bring them together, unite them. They weren't cops and protesters any longer; they were people. Regular people. Folks. It felt . . . like she'd accomplished something good.

With a smile, she pulled Blindspot out of the back of the cruiser and rose off the ground to carry him toward the police station.

"No," Gavriel said. "You walk him. Let them see it, Capitána. Let them see that racist assholes like this guy don't win in the end. He's defeated, by a proud Latina hero. You show them that. Give them a good look."

Annalisa knew some of the people couldn't see him at all, thanks to Blindspot's weird parahuman ability, but many of them could, and everybody could see his muddy footprints beside hers. They cheered her all the way to the police station entrance.

More police officers awaited them inside. A few were white but most were Hispanic or black, and those were the officers who took charge of Blindspot.

"Book him in," Gavriel said with great relish. "I've got a lengthy list of charges to add to his already lengthy list."

A stocky Hispanic lieutenant with tattoos poking out beneath the cuffs of his sleeves whistled for attention. "I want this guy under live guard at all times. If you can see him, you're on the list for monitoring him. If you can't, get back to work because you're not going to help us with him."

"Capitána," a deep voice said, and Annalisa turned to see the Police Chief approaching. "It's nice to see you again, and I'm glad to see you were successful. Catching this guy was a real big deal." His walrus mustache bristled over a smile. "I'm proud to say I know you, and the whole city owes you a debt.

The Mayor has asked if you would come see her when you're done here. She's in the hospital."

Annalisa's face fell. "Oh no! Is she hurt?"

"Just some minor scratches, I assure you. We had a two dozen people wounded in the bomb attacks. The good news is nobody died, and although a couple people's injuries are serious, the prognosis is good for their recovery."

"Okay, so, I guess I should go, then."

"Hold on, I want to say something first. Ladies and gentlemen?" The Chief raised his voice and conversation in the station died down. "I want everyone to know that although she has no legal standing as an officer of the law, I will have La Capitána's name listed as the one making a citizen's arrest in the report, and I fully intend to see her honored for her efforts. Capitána, we salute you." The Chief raised his fingertips to his temple. A moment later, all the officers in the room did likewise.

She felt like she was supposed to say something. "Okay, uh, at ease?"

The station house broke apart in laughter.

"Thanks, you guys," Annalisa said.

"No, thank *you*, Capitána," the Police Chief said.

People were still gathered outside the police station, and as nice as it had been to earn their adulation, Annalisa felt. like she needed a break from it. She checked in with Aighleigh. "Hey, where are you guys now?"

"We're at the hospital," Aighleigh said. "We helped the police secure the area at City Hall and then came here to visit the folks who got hurt. Even Vinnie came, although his head is hurting and he's probably going to go home pretty soon." She paused. "Your police officer friend took some shrapnel."

"Officer Bickle?" Annalisa gasped in dismay. Bickle was such a giant of a man, she hadn't seen how anything could possibly hurt him, even though he didn't have the slightest bit of parahuman power. "Is he . . ."

"He'll be fine. He's in recovery now. If it had been severe, he'd probably still be in surgery."

"I should have—"

"Should have what, Annalisa? You were there, same as all of us. Same as the police. We did everything we could to prevent people from getting hurt, and you even caught Blindspot."

"But people still got hurt!"

"Yes, they did. Maybe if one of us could read minds we could have found him before he placed his bombs. Or if we could travel in time, we could have stopped Dominic Ortega from getting shot. Or maybe we could freeze everyone solid and nobody would ever get hurt again."

"Aighleigh, that's not fair."

"Girl, we both know life isn't fair. We can only do what we can do. We're not failures if we try our hardest and don't succeed. We're failures if we give up and don't try."

"I . . . Darn it, Aighleigh, why do you have to make so much sense?"

"Because I'm trying my hardest. Now are you coming out here to the hospital or are you going to hang around with a bunch of cops all day?"

"No, I'm coming."

"Good." Aighleigh paused. "I need you, Annalisa. I'm . . . I'm barely keeping it together." Annalisa heard the tinge of panic in her friend's voice and suddenly felt guilty for her own selfish fears and uncertainties. Her friend needed her. All her friends did.

"I'm on my way." Annalisa went to the receptionist behind the bulletproof glass. "Hey, is there another way out of this building besides through that door? I'd like to leave without dealing with all those people."

"Of course, Capitána," the woman behind the desk said. "I'll have one of the officers escort you through the garage."

The officer who led Annalisa through the secure entrance to the garage was so young he might barely have been a month or two out of the police academy, and he was star-struck to have a real live superhero in his presence. "I'm a huge fan," he said. "I always wanted to be a superhero but I don't have any powers, and my Musashi test was negative so I never will." They walked past parked cruisers.

Annalisa's own Musashi test, like that of her teammates, had been negative. She said nothing about that, not wanting to give the young man any kind of false hope. "You're still a hero. You're out there protecting and serving." She smiled at him. "Maybe you don't wear spandex, but you can still be one of the good guys."

"Hey . . . You know those two officers who shot Mr. Ortega? We're not all like that."

"I know you're not. It's like any other group. It takes a couple of bad apples to give a bad rap to the whole batch."

The young officer pointed to the tunnel. "You can go through there. There's a security gate, but I guess that doesn't mean anything to someone who can fly. It takes you into a fenced-in lot. You can leave from there."

Annalisa shook the man's hand, careful not to squeeze too hard. "Thank you." She rose into the air and turned toward the tunnel.

"Good luck, Capitána!" he called.

"Same to you!"

Annalisa flew through the tunnel, staying near the ceiling so she wouldn't accidentally run into any incoming vehicles. None came and a moment later, she was blinking in the bright noontime sunlight. The day had grown hot and the sky was a brilliant blue, like the color on travel posters. From horizon to horizon, Annalisa didn't see a single cloud. It made her feel great, and she almost shouted with glee as she launched herself upward.

Chapter Twenty-Nine

"Annalisa!" Aighleigh cried from the wheelchair in which she sat, probably borrowed from the hospital since her quadropede had been damaged when Blindspot attacked City Hall. She and the rest of the Neighborhood Watch waited out front of the hospital, watching the skies along with Chloe and Jacob.

Annalisa dropped to the ground, landing with a solid, reassuring thud. Being back with her friends made her feel powerful, and the look of pride on Jacob's and Chloe's faces uplifted her even more. She grabbed hold of Breezy before he could say anything and planted a big kiss on his lips.

"What the—" he spluttered as Annalisa released him, feeling flushed and excited.

"Just go with it, dude," Cole said. "I'm sure you'll make her mad eventually."

Vinnie snorted with amusement. "I can pretty much guarantee that." After speaking, he lowered his head again, keeping his eyes well shaded from the sunlight.

"Vinnie?" Annalisa asked.

He waved at her. "It's bright out here. I'm not really supposed to be out in it yet."

"Then you should go home, you goof!"

"What, and miss this?"

Aighleigh took one of Vinnie's hands. "I'm calling your mom to come get you."

"She's working. Weekends are big for the suburban tattoo crowd."

"Then I'm calling your dad."

"He's in Atlanta for the X-Games."

"Then I'm calling Breezy's mom."

Vinnie went a little pale. "Oh. Well, my mom would probably come get me if you called her. I'm sure Miss Suzie Homemaker can wait to get her ankle tattoo."

Breezy chuckled. "It's okay, brotha. I'm scared of her too."

"Have you heard how Officer Bickle is doing?" Annalisa asked.

"I asked his partner," Cole said. "She's waiting inside too. She said he's going to be fine."

"You should probably go inside," Aighleigh said. "The Mayor wanted to speak to you, and I know Officer Bickle will want to hear that you got Blindspot."

Chloe and Jacob handed their earbuds back to Aighleigh. "Hey, guys, we really want to thank you for letting us come up here and hang out with you. You guys are a great team and I know you'll be amazing at the Academy. We're going to head back home, though." Chloe gave them all a weak smile. "We're going to be in trouble for coming up here because we're *technically* not quite Just Cause yet . . ."

"They ain't gonna not graduate us or anythin'," Jacob said. "But it's for the best if we don't stick around. Besides, y'all got this well in hand up here. I bet this is the safest town in the country right now with y'all watching over it."

"But what if Cernícala comes back?" Annalisa asked. "She's still out there, somewhere."

"You'll stop her," Chloe said. "You and your team. I bet the five of you could take on pretty much anyone and win. You guys are awesome." Her wings blurred and buzzed as she lifted off the ground. "Message me later, let me know how it's going!" she called over the noise of her wings.

Jacob clasped Breezy's hand, fist-bumped the others, and then accelerated out of the hospital parking lot, heading east toward the highway.

"He is so hot." Cole made his hair ignite, which made the others laugh.

"Easy there, Hothead," Aighleigh said. "You're still underage."

"I'm an overachiever."

"I think he's straight," Annalisa said.

"Oh, I *know* he's straight," Cole said. "I'm also an optimist."

"Are you guys coming in with me?" Annalisa asked the others.

"No, I'll wait out here with Vinnie and get a ride with his mom. I've got to see if my dad can bring his wrecker to pick up my quadropede. It's got a busted leg and I'm back to riding wheels until I fix it," Aighleigh said.

"I'll come in with you, babe," Breezy said.

"Me too," Cole said. "That way we're a walking United Colors of Benetton ad."

Breezy laughed at that and the three young heroes walked into the hospital. A young man in a suit spotted them and got up from his seat quickly, tucking his tablet under his arm. "Ah, Capitána, you're here. The Mayor would like to speak with you."

"Yeah, I heard. Can you tell her I want to check on one of my friends first? One of the officers who was injured."

"Oh, of course." He paused, processing the unexpected request. "Um, can you come back here when you're done and meet me?" He lowered his voice. "I'm just an intern. I don't know how much authority I actually have."

Cole smiled at him. "That's easy. You don't have any at all."

"Yes, we'll be right back as soon as we see Officer Bickle," Annalisa said.

They went through the halls to the recovery wing where they found Bickle sitting in a bed with his left leg bandaged from hip to knee and elevated on a couple pillows. Velez sat in a chair beside him, looking at her phone. She had some scratches on her face but still wore her uniform. She looked up when Annalisa, Breezy, and Cole arrived at the door and Annalisa knocked gently on the door frame.

"Hey, you guys. Bickle, wake your lazy ass up. Company's here."

Bickle opened his eyes and his face broke into a wide smile. "Annalisa! Hey, thank you for coming."

"How are you doing, Officer Bickle?" she asked.

Bickle looked down at himself, wearing a hospital gown over a t-shirt and his elevated leg. "I don't think you get to call me *Officer* when I'm out of uniform. Make it Duane."

"You better still call *me* Officer," Velez said. "I earned that shit."

"Easy, Velez. To answer your question, I'm going to be fine. When one of those devices went off, my leg got peppered with shrapnel. One piece went deep enough to get close to my femoral artery, but it mostly cut meat. I'll be on desk duty for awhile, which means the Lieutenant's going to have to find someone tolerant to work with this feisty chihuahua here."

"Are you gonna have to quit bein' a cop?" Breezy asked. "It's good to have brothers on the force."

"No, but I'll be out of commission for awhile. And to be honest, it's a whole lot better than being dead. I don't know what would have happened if you hadn't spotted that guy and warned us about it. We might be dealing with a bunch of fatalities instead of casualties." Bickle shuddered at the thought. "And I might be one of them. Both of us might be."

"I'm too mean to get killed by the likes of him," Velez said, smiling a predatory grin.

Bickle laughed. "God's truth right there, kids. I heard you got him, Annalisa. I got about a hundred texts about it."

Annalisa looked at her boots, suddenly embarrassed. "Yeah, I guess I did."

"Good. There are only two places where white supremacists belong. In jail or in the ground."

"Do you think I should have . . . have killed him? I could have. I almost did, accidentally."

Breezy gasped at Annalisa's unexpected admission.

Velez shook her head. "No, and I'll tell you why. Say you killed him, and it was in self-defense so nobody in their right mind would charge you with it. That would make you a target for every whacko with an AR-15 and hate for Hispanics. And if they couldn't get you, they'd maybe target someone else. Shoot up a marketplace or a concert or a church. It's happened too many times to count. But you caught him alive, and now he'll go to trial—not just for the crimes he committed today, but for all the other crimes he's wanted for. The media narrative will be him paying for those crimes in a public way, brought to justice by a hero. You, Capitána. A *Latina* hero."

"Won't that still make her a target?" Cole asked.

"It will, but it's also going to embolden other people to stand up, to resist that kind of hateful thinking," Bickle said. "Bullies and haters are cowards. They fold when people stand up to them. This is how we root that shit—sorry, my bad. This is how we root that stuff out of our society. We show people it doesn't fly with us anymore, and anyone who perpetrates it is going to suffer severe penalties."

"I'm glad you didn't kill him," Velez said.

"Me too," Breezy said. "I don't want a girlfriend who's a killer."

"Oh, are you two an item now? *Quelle surprise.* I guess the cat's . . ." Cole yawned. "Out of the bag."

"Any sign of Cernícala?" Annalisa asked, pointedly ignoring Cole's needling.

"That *chica* who shot us up yesterday? No, no sign of her. Maybe she got what she wanted when the Mayor had Phelps and Hembeck arrested," Velez said.

"I hope she's in the wind," Breezy said.

"I hope I get one more crack at her," Velez retorted. "Just one punch. I'll show her how afraid I am."

"Anyway, Duane, I'm glad you're going to be okay."

"Me too, Annalisa. Thanks for coming by to check on me."

"I don't know a lot of police officers, and you guys are . . . you're my friends."

Velez snorted in contempt but managed to look pleased nevertheless.

"The Mayor said she wanted to talk to me."

"Well, you best not keep Her Honor waiting," Bickle said. "Take care, you guys. And for the love of God, take the rest of the weekend off. You've earned it."

"We will," Cole said. "At least, as much as we can." He winked. "We have a town to keep safe. Annalisa, you need us with you to see the Mayor?"

"No, I think I can handle her."

Cole snickered. "I meant to protect her from you."

Chapter Thirty

The others headed back to help with cleanup at City Hall, and Annalisa promised she would join them as soon as she was done speaking with the Mayor. She rapped her knuckles on the door frame of the diagnosis room the nurse led her to. "Come in, Annalisa," Mayor Babcock said. She was sitting up in the bed. She wasn't wearing a gown, instead retaining the professional attire she'd worn for the press conference, although her jacket was folded over the back of the room chair and she had bandages over her bare arm and another on her cheek.

"You're hurt . . ." Annalisa said.

Babcock smiled, even though Annalisa could clearly see it hurt her to do so. "I'll be just fine. My injuries are really superficial. I'll have some interesting scars to tell my grandchildren about someday. Thanks to you and your friends, I'm going to have another chance to do that."

"Oh." Annalisa realized she'd just been thanked. "Uh, you're welcome."

"The past few days have been very difficult for me, both personally and as Mayor. Yes, I know they've been hard for everyone, and I'm not trying to minimize anyone else's experiences. As Mayor, I need to represent the will of the people of this city— not just those who elected me, but everyone who didn't as well. I know I wasn't elected on a strong minority rights platform." She snorted with acrid amusement. "I was elected because the other guy was a crook. Maybe that only means I'm the lesser of two evils. At least nobody was chanting *lock her up* about me during the campaign. Do you follow me?"

Annalisa thought about it. "Yeah, I think I do."

"I know this is a white town. We don't have a lot of Hispanics, and not many black families at all. Because of that, race hasn't been a big issue for me, and probably not for a lot of people. We just don't think about it, because every day, we mostly see people who look just like us."

"White," Annalisa said, and it wasn't a question. She knew it was true. Her school was, demographically, very similar to the rest of the town in terms of racial makeup.

"And that is my failing. Racial tolerance isn't just for towns with large minority populations. Huh. *Minority.* That's an outdated term, Annalisa. I don't like the implication that a group of people is somehow less important. In fact, I'm going to make a conscious effort not to use that term anymore. People are *people*, and that's what they should be first, last, and in between."

"That sounds like a really good idea to me, but I don't know if you'll get a lot of people to agree with you." Annalisa lowered her voice. "Just because you don't *say* minority doesn't mean we won't be thought of that way. Or treated that way."

"I know, and that's what I mean is my failing. I know I'm just one mayor in a small town in one state, but if I can make the smallest difference here, maybe some other mayor in another town will make a difference. And then maybe a governor will. And maybe, if enough of us do, we can push back the forces of fear and hatred and start listening to each other and trusting each other again." She paused and took a sip of water from the cup beside her bed. "Come Monday, I'm going to get with the council. We'll start working on a program for government employees, for law enforcement personnel. Something that will help us listen, and trust, and treat *everyone* like people, no matter who they are."

Annalisa smiled. "Thank you, Mayor. That means a lot." She didn't know if the Mayor would manage it or not, but an honest effort to change for the better was positive.

"I know you and your friends will be leaving us soon to go to the Hero Academy, and that is to the detriment of this town. It will be less safe without the five of you in it. We will have to persevere. I'm grateful for your efforts today and in days past. You have undoubtedly saved many lives, and wherever you and your friends wind up, please know that you will always have a home here in Loveland." The Mayor smiled again. "Ouch. I really need to stop doing that. The other thing I will be addressing with the council is some sort of recognition for the five of you. It's important, especially in this political environment, that those parahumans who are the heroes, the *helpers*, are recognized for their efforts."

"You don't have to do that, Mayor."

"No, I don't. It's the things we don't have to do but do anyway that are the most meaningful."

Annalisa smiled. "I wasn't sure about you at first, Mayor, but you're all right. If I was eighteen, I'd vote for you."

Mayor Babcock chuckled. "Oh, ow. Ow. Thank you, Annalisa. And please, thank your friends. I will have someone from my office get in touch with the five of you very soon. For now, though, I think I need to stop talking. My face hurts."

"I'm sorry you got hurt."

"I'm sorry lots of people got hurt, and sorry Mr. Ortega got killed. I will do my best to make sure it doesn't happen again here in this city."

"I'll do my best, too. We all will."

"I know, Annalisa." Babcock leaned back on the bed and shut her eyes, clearly exhausted from her injuries.

Annalisa stepped out of the room, not knowing what she should do next. She smiled at a young Hispanic woman with disheveled hair sitting on a bench in the hallway. The young woman smiled back in a distracted sort of way, like she wasn't really paying attention to anything in particular.

Annalisa took another step and froze. Something about the woman wasn't quite right. She looked familiar. She looked back and the woman's face fell and she knew she'd been made.

Cernícala.

The woman stood, looking both directions up the hall as if to decide which was the best way to flee.

"Cernícala . . ." Annalisa said, pitching her voice low enough so it wouldn't carry further than the woman's ears. "Can we talk? Just talk."

Cernícala froze. Annalisa saw a struggle playing out on her face, which was framed by dirty, stringy hair in need of a good shampooing. Her clothes were worn and dirty as well. She gave off the same vibe as the homeless people Annalisa sometimes saw standing at the corners of intersections with their cardboard signs. "Talk?" the woman asked.

Annalisa raised her hands and opened them. "Just talk. No fighting. No chasing. You're faster than me anyway, and I'm tired."

Cernícala curled her lip in suspicion, chewing on one corner of her mouth, but nodded. "Where?"

"The roof? Nobody will interrupt us up there." She followed Cernícala out the main entrance. The young woman immediately launched herself into the sky, catching Annalisa off guard.

Annalisa glanced around, but nobody was pointing and shouting. Maybe nobody had seen Cernícala. She flew up to the roof, more than half expecting the supervillain would be gone, streaking away at a pace she couldn't match. Instead, she was sitting with her back to an air conditioning unit and watched as Annalisa landed in front of her.

"What do you want to talk about?" Cernícala asked without preamble.

"Why are you here? I figured you'd be long gone by now," Annalisa said.

Cernícala's facade of bravado showed some cracks. "I—I'm not sure why. I saw what you did, back at City Hall. I was watching to see what the Mayor would say about those two murderers."

"The officers who killed Mr. Ortega are being charged with it."

"I know. That's good. That's a win."

"But you still didn't leave?"

"No, because that's when that *puto* Blindspot showed up and set off his bombs." Her voice went sharp. "I hate him so much. He follows me around."

"He's not following you. He's following the protests, just like you are."

"That's *different*," Cernícala said. "Cops killed my brother."

"Maybe someone killed Blindspot's brother."

"He had a brother?"

Annalisa shrugged. "I don't know. But he's a white dude who's invisible to other white people. That's probably messed him up somehow. I know that's no excuse for him, but I'm just trying to say that everyone has issues."

"Okay, fine. We're all screwed up. Is that your professional superhero opinion or are you just an *amateur*?" Cernícala spat the last word and waited, as if she were trying to get a rise out of Annalisa.

Annalisa didn't take the bait, even though she wanted to. *Oh* did she *ever*. "You know what your problem is, Cernícala?"

"Oh, I've just got one? Do tell." Cernícala crossed her arms.

"You're not solving anything. You're a Hispanic parahuman, like me. You've got that going for you. You could be so much more than just a . . . a parapowered bully who shoots at cops."

"I told you, cops killed my brother!"

"*One* cop. I read your file. Not every cop is like that. Most of them are just like anyone else. They go to their job and get through their shift and go home. They're not out there looking for people to shoot." Annalisa crossed her arms, parroting Cernícala's pose. "Unlike you."

Cernícala opened her mouth to say something, but the words clearly backed up in her throat as Annalisa's final statement penetrated her brain.

"You could help defuse these tense situations between police and protesters. Help them find some common ground. Help them understand one another. Get them talking with each other instead of screaming at each other."

Cernícala shook her head. "It would never work. People want to hurt each other."

Annalisa sighed. "I'm really sorry you feel that way, Cristina."

Cernícala blinked. "What did you call me?"

"Cristina. That's your name, isn't it? I'm Annalisa. I'd offer to shake your hand, but you don't trust me."

Suddenly, tears spilled down Cernícala's cheeks, and Annalisa didn't know why. "What's wrong?"

Cernícala wiped her eyes. "*Lo siento*. It's just that . . . nobody's said my name to me for a long time. It's hard to hear it."

"You shut everyone out. You've been on this big crusade against the police, but all it's doing is tying you up in knots. You need to stop hating. Give yourself permission to unwind."

Cernícala broke down entirely, crying like she'd been saving it up for years. Maybe she had, Annalisa thought. She knew how the conversation would have to end, and she was dreading it, but maybe she could make it a little less painful. She stepped forward and put tentative arms around Cernícala in a gentle embrace. The young woman tensed for a moment, then gave herself over to it and allowed herself to sob against Annalisa's shoulder.

"It'll be okay," Annalisa said. "You've had a hard time."

"I'm just so tired. All I ever do is chase the protests."

"Cristina . . . I know it's been rough for you, and I'm really sorry, but I can't let you just leave."

"Wh-what? But we've been . . . talking . . ."

"I know. And we can talk some more, but you hurt some people yesterday, and you could have killed the people in that helicopter if I hadn't been able to save them."

Cernícala bowed her head. "I didn't mean for that to happen."

"I know you didn't, but it did, and like my Mamá says, there are consequences." Annalisa released Cernícala from her embrace. "I don't want to have to fight you or chase you, because I think more than anything you need help, and maybe we can find you some."

For a moment, Annalisa thought the young woman would fly off, and she really was too tired to pursue Cernícala if she bolted. Then she slumped. "What am I supposed to do?"

Annalisa canted her head toward the parking lot below where Bickle's and Velez's cruiser was parked. "I have a couple of police officer friends. One of them got hurt from Blindspot's bombs and his partner is sitting with him. Will you turn yourselves in to them? I'll go with you. I'll make sure you get treated . . . with dignity."

Cernícala nodded. "All right."

Chapter Thirty-One

Thursday, May 28, 2020
Loveland, CO

"Free at last!" Aighleigh crowed as she rolled off the bus from Malley Middle School for the last time. Annalisa high-fived her, then slipped her hand into Breezy's. She'd found herself feeling more clingy as they reached the end of the school year. It was silly, she told herself. Breezy wasn't going anywhere and neither was she. They'd be around all summer except for Annalisa's regular July camping trip with her parents, and then they'd start school at the Hero Academy together in August. They'd get four more years together, and maybe longer if they were lucky enough to get assigned to the same team. And who knew . . . if they stayed together long enough to get really serious, well, they wouldn't be the first married heroes. Mustang Sally and Mastiff—before he died. Crackerjack and Desert Eagle. Even the principal and the Dean of Students at the Hero Academy were married—MetalBlade and Icebreaker.

Still, they were only fourteen, and the future was a long way off. In the meantime, they had a graduation party to have at the Neighborhood Watch Headquarters. With them all moving on to the Academy, it also felt like the end of the Neighborhood Watch era. Annalisa and Aighleigh had spent several long evenings talking about that while Aighleigh sweated over the repairs on her quadropede. It was going to be a lot harder to leave that part behind, like the team was being decommissioned. That was Aighleigh's word, and Annalisa had to look it up on her dictionary app.

"It's not really the end of the Watch," Annalisa said. "We're not retiring. We're moving up to the big leagues. We'll still be superheroes, and if we're lucky, we'll get to stay together after the Academy when the PRA people see how good we are together." She and the others walked up to the entrance of the scrap yard. They turned the corner and stopped in their tracks.

The yard was full of people. Not customers looking to pull parts, but regular people. There were big folding tables set up, with table cloths covered with food—chips, salads, coolers full of drinks. Three grills were going at one end of the yard, manned by Torvald's husband Carson, who was an amazing chef. Torvald was there too, chatting with Vinnie's heavily tattooed and pierced mother. Annalisa saw Mayor Babcock, dressed down in shorts and a t-shirt with *Neighborhood Watch* printed on it. In fact, a lot of people were wearing similar shirts, like officers Bickle and Velez, whom she almost didn't recognize without their uniforms.

Annalisa didn't have to see who whistled like he was calling a cab. That was her dad, who could make himself heard over the sound of a jackhammer when he tried. People began to applaud and cheer for the young heroes. Annalisa leaned down to Aighleigh. "Did you know about this?" A forest of arms holding camera phones extended toward them.

"No!" Aighleigh looked utterly mystified that her father had somehow managed to keep an event of this magnitude a complete secret.

"Hey, my dad's here!" Vinnie said, sounding pleased. He stood nearby, rocking a massive beard and rocking back and forth on a skateboard while he and Aighleigh's dad shared a joke.

A woman stepped forward, raising her hands for quiet, and the raucous crowd settled down. "Isn't that the news reporter you saved from the helicopter? Heather something?" Cole asked.

Annalisa nodded, and she realized Marlon the pilot was standing behind her. He smiled and raised his bottle the same way he had from the back of the ambulance the last time she'd seen him.

"Everyone, thank you all for coming today. We're here to recognize and honor the superheroes of the Neighborhood Watch, and to thank them for their years spent protecting this sleepy little town," Heather the reporter said. "Many of us in some way owe our very lives to you and your efforts, myself included." She raised her bottle. "We are grateful. To the Neighborhood Watch!"

"To the Neighborhood Watch!" the rest of the gathered people replied.

Mayor Babcock stepped forward to stand beside the pilot. "Aighleigh, Annalisa, Cole, Vinnie, Breezy . . . I am so grateful to have had the opportunity to meet each of you and to see firsthand the kind of work you've done to protect the people of Loveland. I've found it inspiring, and to that end, I and the rest of the council have been working closely with the police department to create the Neighborhood Watch Initiative. It's designed to increase communication between government and civilians, to educate and inform about issues of race and prejudice, and to teach law enforcement personnel to respond first with kindness and words instead of threats and violence. We may not solve it overnight, but I hope this is the first step of many in the right direction. I owe it to the five of you."

More applause broke out and Annalisa felt she was being lifted into the air by a string. She wasn't a superhero for the adulation—she would do it even if it was from behind a mask and nobody knew it was her. Being recognized for what she did felt nice. She squeezed Breezy's hand. "Come on, Breezy, let's go get a burger while Carson's still manning the grill."

Aighleigh's dad intercepted them before they got very far across the yard. "Hey . . . I'm not much for speeches. You know that. But a couple of your friends from Just Cause stopped by to drop something off. They said they couldn't stay and they apologized. It sounds like they had to report to their teams or something. Anyway, Aighleigh, they said this is for you." He pulled a black plastic tarp off something mechanical. For a moment, Annalisa thought it was a new quadropede, and she was partly correct.

The device unfolded itself from a tightly-compacted ball to stand upon four sturdy but graceful legs. Its back was arched to form a natural saddle, and it raised an elongated head with glowing eyes and other sensory devices mounted upon it. It was a robotic . . .

"Horse," Cole said. "Cool."

"Oh-h-h," Aighleigh breathed. "I know what this is. It's the Destroyer tech. Chloe and Jacob told me about it. I didn't know they would actually get hold of it."

Aighleigh's dad handed her an envelope. It was addressed to *Cavalier*. Aighleigh slid her finger through the seal and pulled out a letter. "It's mine," she said after a moment. "Like, really mine. They *gave* it to me. Just Cause did. It's signed by Snapdragon. He's the commander of Just Cause Denver."

"Wait, does this mean we ain't gonna call you *Wheels* no more?" Breezy asked around a mouthful of hamburger. Apparently his hunger had gotten the best of him and he'd managed to acquire one without letting go of Annalisa's hand, the sly fox.

"What's *Cavalier* mean?" Vinnie asked.

"It means you need to read more," Aighleigh said with a laugh. "Annalisa, help me onto this thing. I want to try it out."

"Are you sure it's safe?" Annalisa asked. "I mean, Destroyer made it, right? He was a supervillain."

Cole flexed his eyebrows and tendrils of smoke shot up from both of them. "So? We're the Neighborhood Watch. We've fought supervillains since we were kids. A stupid robotic horse isn't going to get the best of us."

Vinnie burst out laughing and high-fived his dad, who had ambled over to watch the proceedings.

Annalisa lifted Aighleigh from her chair and carefully sat her upon the saddle. "Don't fall."

Safety straps emerged from the horse's sides and back to secure her friend upon the saddle. "Oh-h-h," Aighleigh said again. "I already like this.

Dad, I'm going to need another container. Unless you want to let me bring the horse into the house."

"You are not bringing that thing into my house," her father said. "Even I have some standards."

People laughed.

Annalisa watched as the people in the crowd laughed and ate and talked with one another. All different ages and colors and genders, just getting along. It felt like a victory at last. Like Mayor Babcock had said, maybe they wouldn't solve all the problems overnight . . .

. . . but it was a first step in the right direction.

Author Notes

I have been lax in recent books about thanking those who have helped me to bring them to fruition, and I don't want to let that slip by again. I am tremendously grateful to my beta readers Adrienne, Chris, and Ira, all of whom brought their unique viewpoints to help me find the story amid all these words. Scott Story has once again put pen to paper and come up with a dynamite cover which gives Annalisa all the majesty and power she deserves. Truly, the man is a wizard and I'm lucky to have him doing covers for me. My family —completely against their better judgment— continues to support this crazy writing habit of mine, and I'm thankful for them.

Finally, I want to thank all of you, the fans, for continuing to buy, read, and review my books. Without knowing you are out there, anxious for more stories in the Just Cause Universe, I would find it a lot harder to keep coming up with new ones.

-Ian Healy, February 9, 2019

ABOUT THE AUTHOR

Ian Thomas Healy dabbles in many different genres. He's a fourteen-time participant and winner of National Novel Writing Month. He created the popular ongoing superhero series, the *Just Cause Universe*, and is also the creator of the *Writing Better Action Through Cinematic Techniques* workshop, which helps writers to improve their action scenes.

When not writing, which is rare, he enjoys watching hockey, reading comic books (and serious books, too), and living in the great state of Colorado, which he shares with his wife, children, house-pets, and approximately five million other people.

Visit *www.ianthealy.com* for more information.